Spare Parts

Big City Tales

Michael J Phillips

Published by Michael J Phillips

https://michaeljphillips.co.uk/

Michael J Phillips on Facebook

Thanks to
My Wife Karen for her patience and understanding.
Leoni Delgado and Mike Sullivan for allowing me to pick their brains.

Special thanks to Michelle Emerson for her kind words of encouragement and knowledge.

Contents

Jasper and the Jump Guy

Part I

So, I'm in the Monkey Tree staring at The Jump Guy. It's fair to say he is being as frustratingly annoying as usual.

'Did you hear from her, Jasper?' he asks me.

'No,' I say.

'Ah, you would have thought she'd text you. No missed calls or WhatsApp messages either?'

'No, besides which she doesn't have my number!'

I sigh heavily after my firm response. He glances at the floor and then at his cold pint of lager on the bar. He licks his lips and lifts the vessel.

'She's a fool. That's all I have to say on the subject.'

Of course, I know it's far from the last thing he will have to say. The Jump Guy always has something to say, normally about me and my love life. It distracts him from thinking about his own. He throws a large splash of the amber fluid down his throat.

'Maybe you need to go back to the club and try again. She'd be mad as a box of frogs not to say yes if you ask her out.'

'A box of frogs?'

The Jump Guy smirks.

'Yeah, a fucking large box too!'

I laugh weakly.

'Maybe.'

'Definitely maybe! Remember fortune favours the brave.'

'Jeez! I never had you down as a cliché type of guy. Where did you learn that?'

'Tipping Point, I think … or was it The Chase? Can't remember now.'

The server carries a tray of fish and chips past me and to a young couple sitting in the corner. The pair look vibrant as they smile at the waiter with glee.

I nod to the landlord, Baz.

'Two pints of Uri please Baz.'

Margie slips from behind the bar and sidles up to me, gently patting my backside as usual.

'You hungry, lovely boy?'

Margie felt it her duty to ensure that all her punters were well fed, but it came at a cost, of course.

'I'm good, thanks, Margie. I had a Clarkie earlier.'

'A pie?! That's all you've had today?'

I think back to our conversation when I arrived earlier. The Jump Guy hadn't come in yet, and Margie was interrogating me.

'You seen anything of Jimmy?'

'The Jump Guy? He'll be in soon.'

"I'm a bit worried about him. He doesn't seem right at the moment.'

'He has never been right if you ask me,' Baz had chipped in.

'You leave him alone,' she barked back.

'Well, you can both ask him yourselves later,' I advised.

That was a good hour ago now. The Jump Guy arrived a short while later and was now in full flight.

I have vague memories of first meeting him. It was in a nightclub on Mill Lane. I remember him collecting his winnings from one of the fruities. At that moment, the only thing we had in common was being as drunk as ten Lords. I have learned loads about him since then. Jimmy the Jump Guy is easy-going and a bit of a lady's man. He loves women, in fact, and they love him. He likes a drink, smokes like several large industrial chimneys, and wears the look of an eighties football casual. At six foot two, he can appear intimidating to some. He's not though, trust me. He loves his Stone Island clobber, and always has a pair of Adidas Trimm-Trabbs adorning his feet. The Jump Guy isn't a local lad, though; he came down from Manchester back in the nineties, running away from something or someone, no doubt. He also has a gift; vast knowledge of the gee-gees, and the jumps are his area of expertise. He has no time for flat racing, which he always describes as like watching someone mow a lawn badly. I wish I could understand what that means. The Jump Guy finishes his beer and barks at Baz.

'Line them up, Baz, mate, and get us a couple of tequila slammers too. Had a good day at the bookies today.'

The drinks appear in double-quick time; the pub grows busier. The fish and chip couple in the corner have been replaced by a noisy hen party. There is lots of giggling from the women as the bride-to-be glugs a glass of Prosecco. She chases it down with a sambuca shot. Her L-Plates fall to the floor as she slams the empty glass on the table. Her heel pierces one of them as she stumbles. I can sense the oncoming carnage. I swear I can hear the four horsemen of the apocalypse screeching up outside. I look at the tequila now placed in front of me; this isn't good. I try to distract myself.

'So, what's new, you been good?'

The Jump Guy wriggles slightly in his seat,

'Yeah ok. Well, no … that's not strictly true actually.'

'You being chased for money again?'

'Nope.'

'Is it a woman?'

'Well, not exactly.'

'Is it a married woman?'

'Fucking hell, Jasper! I have some morals, you know!"

'Ha!!!! Morals?! You?!'

'Fuck you!'

'Ok, Ok. I'm sorry … go on.'

'Just some shit from back home. It'll get sorted.'

I leave it at that. More drinks arrive. We both fall silent for a moment before The Jump Guy starts a mini pity party.

> 'To be honest, Jasper, there's no such thing as love. It's a myth. I ain't ever had it or known it. Don't get me wrong, I've tried it. Hell, I even thought I was in love once, way back in the day. Yeah, I really did. Couldn't wait to see her, butterflies in my stomach and all that. I even wrote her a poem, gave her flowers, dinner dates and all that Mills and Boon shit. And then one day she fucked off with my best mate. I figure that whoever you love, they end up leaving you one way or another. It's all a crock of shit, and they can keep it, whoever they are! Love is just something invented by florists and card sellers, I reckon.'

I think hard on his words as the tequila swims around my head.

'It'll happen when you least expect it,' I tell him.

'When heaven freezes over!'

'Hell,' I correct.

The Jump Guy surveys the mayhem in the pub. Two members of the hen party are now fighting, and the bride-to-be is crying. A man is kicking the fruit machine whilst his drunken mate doubles up laughing.

'Yeah, you're right. Let's get out of here.'

And so, we head into the neon lights of the night.

Part II

Brandii's day was getting worse as it went on. Her hairdryer had burnt out, she had stubbed her toe on the leg of the bed, and now the batteries had gone in her vibrator. The final straw came when she laddered her last pair of stockings. It wasn't ideal at the best of times, of course, but on a Saturday, her busiest day, it was cataclysmic. Her one saving grace was that her next client wasn't due for another two hours, which gave her plenty of time to sort herself out. The client was a regular who simply booked himself in as Mr X, but she knew who he was, so much so that she had given him a nickname. The Naked Accountant was heavily into S&M, among various other 'left-field' activities. She had given him that moniker because he looked like an accountant. He always turned up in a black suit, white shirt, and black tie. He wore highly polished black shoes with a black leather briefcase clamped under his arm. Brandii liked him, though, he was always so polite, and it was easy money too; and that was almost certainly the best kind. You couldn't beat it, although she regularly beat him.

Spenders was a Whore House, Cat House, Brothel, Knocking Shop, Bordello and Bawdy House. Those were just some of the monikers people chose to label it with. To be fair, Brandii never really gave a toss what people called it. When she wasn't working, it doubled as her home, a home provided by Frank and Ethel Cartwright, the proprietors of Spenders. Brandii wasn't her proper name, of course. She grew up a young girl from the Rhymney Valleys, real name Sally-Anne Elias. She lived an innocent life until one day, it stopped being so innocent. Her father started beating her whenever he had been drinking, which was most days by then. Her mother did nothing to stop it; too afraid, she supposed. So, eventually, she ran away. Sally-Anne wound up homeless in Cardiff. It was tough and got even tougher the night someone tried to beat her up and rob her. Luckily, her attacker was frightened off by a woman dressed like a fifties movie star. Smartly dressed in a shiny grey jacket with a matching pencil skirt, Ethel Cartwright planted her umbrella over the attacker's head with elegance and aplomb. She spun the umbrella in the air end to end and then rapped the bamboo handle across the attacker's head once again; she defended Sally-Anne with grace. Ethel looked after her from that point on. She certainly never encouraged or forced Sally-Anne into the profession; it just happened seamlessly over time. And so, Sally-Anne became Brandii; a beautiful, sweet, and kind piece of damaged goods; she wasn't the only one out there.

Despite the mishaps that beset Brandii today, it had been a funny kind of a day too. She had an older married couple in earlier on, which was a rarity indeed. It was another easy gig for her too. She just sat there whilst the couple got down to it. They stripped off and started having sex at full pelt, whilst she just watched. They seemed oblivious to her being present. Brandii never ceased to marvel at how people got their rocks off; but if that was what the client asked for, then who was she to demur? In a perverted way, clients like this backed up her theory that what she did was a form of relationship counselling.

The day had now moved on into the night, and lamplit shadows hit the blinds of her room. The Naked Accountant had come (quite literally) and gone. It wouldn't be long before her last client turned up now. Just the very thought of seeing him made her heart leap. She knew it was wrong ethically and realised that she had committed a cardinal sin; she had fallen in love with this man. He was more to her than a client or punter. She wasn't sure he felt the same way, though. But he came to see her twice a week, and that could only be a good thing, couldn't it?

It all started when he turned up drunk off the street one night, looking for a girl. Ethel suggested Brandii to him. She remembered how he grunted and then let her lead him to her room. But he wasn't interested in sex, he just wanted to talk whilst he lay in her arms. Sometimes he would pour forth his most intimate secrets. Brandii identified with him immediately, more damaged goods, of course, but she could fix him. So she just let him talk; she listened to his amplified thoughts. Brandii reckoned it was only a matter of time until he realised how much she was prepared to be there for him; to heal him. Then and only then could they move on to the new life she had been dreaming of. Yes, she couldn't wait to see him tonight.

Part III

We rock up slowly to the entrance to Maddigans. I note that Brad and Tony look particularly menacing tonight.

'Try not to agitate them,' I whisper to the Jump Guy. He grabs me by the shoulder,

> 'They're just a pair of jumped-up gorillas, Jasper, mate. In fact, that is detrimental to the intelligence of gorillas.'

Brad and Tony flex their muscly arms across their chests as we approach. They stand defensively with a single earpiece strapped to both their heads. The burly pair chew gum faster than an amphetamine-fuelled cow chewing grass. Both have the same hairstyle too. *They probably go to the same gym and tanning shop also,* I reason in my head.

Brad nods at the Jump Guy as we arrive at the door,

'You going to keep an eye on him, Jasper? We don't want a repeat of last time, do we?'

'I can vouch for him Brad. You know that.'

'Yeah, but who will vouch for you, you little shit?' teases Tony.

The doorman's words fill me with dread. They always do. I know he is trying to scare me; it works every time, and he knows this. He slaps me on the back as I enter. My lungs heave back and forth from the impact.

We stumble into the club, the tequila slammers having now worn off from earlier. I like it here. It caters for all ages. In one corner, there could be couples in their fifties who had never stopped coming to town just because they got married or hit a certain age, people who had never given up on dancing in the moonlight. Dotted around the club are hen dos, stag dos, hag dos, shag dos and anyone-will-dos. The place has a jukebox and regular live music too. It is a jewel in St Mary Street's crown.

We battle our way to the bar. I employ my periscope impression and stand on tip-toe, peering above the crowd. In all honesty, I look more like an expectant meerkat with piles. I spot Roisin immediately. Her red hair dances around her head; she smiles and laughs with the punters whilst pulling pints or pouring spirits. For a brief moment, I wonder if her name actually is Roisin. Her name badge tells me she is, and I have no reason to disbelieve that piece of information unless she has borrowed the badge from someone else. Maybe she isn't called Roisin; maybe she is called Maybelline or Doris; not that it matters, I have an aunty called Doris. She is a lovely woman, although I find it hard to imagine her pouring pints. Roisin catches my eye as she serves a small group of Japanese tourists. They all want a pint of Brains Dark; tourists being tourists. Roisin glimpses over at me. Her smile and nod reassure me that I am to be served next. I can't contain my grin as she carefully pours out a couple of beers. Minutes later, I find myself cradling the lovingly poured drink with the Jump Guy. I take a sip, look around, and then decide to tackle him again.

'Penny for them.'

He laughs defensively,

'Cost you more than that!'

I shrug my shoulders back at him,

'What's going on? You know you can tell me anything.'

'Fuck all. Now, how did you get on?'

'When?'

'Then, with your lady behind the bar.'

'You mean Roisin?'

'Roisin! Oh, we're on first name terms now, are we?'

The Jump Guy laughs again and slugs the rest of his drink down. He heads purposefully back to the bar.

I watch from afar as he orders more drinks from Roisin. She laughs as she serves him. I can't help but notice how many women check the Jump Guy out as he stands at the bar. One girl backs away from the bar and starts dancing up to him; the Human League's 'Don't You Want Me?' fills the air as she does so. I tap my foot to it; it's a great tune, after all. Jimmy smiles back at her as he begins his swagger back to me. If only the dancing girl realised what a troubled soul he really is. If only I knew what a troubled soul he is.

'I warned her not to serve you again, Jasper, told her you were wanted by Interpol, and it was only a matter of time before they caught up with you. Told her they wanted you for your poor taste in clothes and that receding hairline.'

'Bastard!'

He laughs briefly; a frown then returns to his face. I wish I could take it away for him with a swipe of my hand, but I can't.

We find ourselves outside Dorothy's in Chip Alley. It has just gone 11pm. The road busies itself with revellers. I stand with my tray of chips, smiling stupidly into the distance. I'd done it. I managed to get a date with her. My persistence had paid off; Roisin had consented to meet me for dinner and a few drinks. I am truly elated. I can't say the same for the Jump Guy, though. He sucks on a cigarette; I realise he just wants to go home, or maybe he has other ideas. We eventually go our separate ways.

Part IV

The wee-wee hours creep along quietly. The Jump Guy lays awake with Brandii by his side. He lights another cigarette and reaches out for the stale whisky glass at the side of the bed. Brandii gently strokes his chest with her pink-tipped fingernails.

'You need to sleep, Jimmy. So do I as it goes.'

'I'm not stopping you.'

She sits up and takes the cigarette from him. Inhaling gently, she hands it back. 'Why don't we go and do something today? I got the day off. We could go for a picnic maybe?'

'Me and you? A Picnic?'

'Yeah, why not? Let's go to Roath Park or Cosmeston Lakes, maybe? It'll be something different.'

'Nah, I got something on later.'

'What about after that? We could go for food?'

The Jump Guy empties his glass. He refills it slowly.

'Do you believe in love, Brandii?'

'Course I do, doesn't everyone?'

'Don't be daft. It's a fucking myth.'

Brandii's heart sinks briefly. But she is hopeful that she can show him it is real. She feels it, and she feels it for him so much.

'But you must have been in love at some time, Jimmy?'

He laughs momentarily,

'With myself, maybe.'

Brandii giggles back,

'Well, no one could blame you for that. You're gorgeous you are, well lush.'

He puts his arm around her and pulls her tight to his chest,

'What about you? You been in love with anyone?'

Her moment has arrived. She feels that it is her time to put it out there; to let him know,

'I am now as it goes.'

'Really?! Does he know? Or is it a woman? I shouldn't presume really, should I?'

Brandii gulps so hard it almost tears the skin off the inside of her throat. Her pulse quickens, her heart edges nearer to exploding.

'It's you, Jimmy. I love you.'

*****

The front of Central Station is bedecked with a mix of homeless people and drunken stragglers. One side with no home to go to; the other with homes they can't get to; not until the trains start anyway. The early morning has brought light rain, but it is showing signs of clearing. A dishevelled man with a beard as long as his arms approaches the Jump Guy for a cigarette and the price of a cup of tea. He flips a few pound coins back at the man, along with a partially full packet of cigarettes. The man bows his head and puts his hands together.

'Namaste, my friend,' he utters.

It is decision time again for the Jump Guy. He has never been one for responsibility. In fact, the moment it walks in the room, he runs for the exit. He knows it's not right to keep running away but he can't be helped. He has been doing so for years, and he is getting tired of it now, exhausted, in fact. He thinks back to Brandii's words, but it wouldn't be fair on her in the long run because he can't commit to anything but the inevitable, his own self-destruction. Love will never be on the cards for him because he is his own worst enemy. His time is done here now. This town had taken the best of him and not given much back in return. It is a thankless and seemingly empty quest; a search for something that is probably never going to be found, not in this life anyway. The race is run now, and he feels like he has been pipped at the post again.

The Jump Guy realises that running away can never hide or heal the scars of his past, though. He knows the time has come to make another vacuous journey to another town, or maybe he can just go home. He enters the station concourse and looks up at the choice of destinations on the trailblazers. New destinations flash at him, the world is his, but he doesn't know what to do with it. He notices there is a train to Manchester leaving shortly, his hometown. There is always that option, but it is last on his list. He takes one last look through the door at the city street; he's had an alright time here, albeit a sometimes lonely one. He heads to the ticket machine.

Kitchens

I am watching Ginny as she reads the paper. Her cup of tea is well on its way to going cold as she engrosses herself in another celebrity scandal. I find it hard to break my gaze as I sip at my cooling brew. I scrutinise her visage, skin so flawless surrounded by long raven hair. Try as I might, I cannot get a glimpse of her honey-brown eyes; they are fixed solidly on the words she is reading. I wonder how many times I have kissed those lips. I know it is more than one hundred; it must be. What am I thinking about? It has to be at least a thousand, ten thousand even. I sigh slowly.

> 'Bloody hell, Vic, what you sighing about? Always bloody sighing you are.'

I sigh again; even if I have kissed them over a hundred thousand times, it still isn't enough. Ginny always complains that I'm not right; why wasn't I like normal men, she'd say to me, why wasn't I off fishing or playing golf? Point is, I don't want to go anywhere without her. Anyway, I hate fishing, and if anyone had ever seen me try to play golf, they'd know why I hate that too. I get up from the creaky chair and put the kettle on. She lets out a gentle cough,

> 'Nothing on the bloody TV tonight again. I don't know why we bother with a licence!'
>
> 'We could go out?' I offer.
>
> 'No, why don't you go out instead? Give your brother a ring and go to the snooker hall or for a couple of pints with him. I'll be fine here.'

I sigh again; she rustles her paper a bit harder.

The kettle gives a gentle clicking sound as it reaches its climax. I place the fresh cup of tea next to her and note that she has moved on to the crossword now. I look over her shoulder in

a vain attempt to help her. She is having none of it, though. She pulls the paper from my view. I sit and sigh again. She places the paper flat on the table, looking as studious as the keenest fresher at Oxford or Cambridge. I notice the patch of condensation on the ceiling. It has become a total eyesore now. No matter how many times I promise to get it sorted, my mind refuses to remind me.
Ginny coughs.

'Five down, seven letters, the clue is "suffocated"?'

I feel quite honoured to be asked,

'Any letters?'

'Begins with an S and the fourth letter is an F.'

I get a wave of excitement,

'Stifled!'

'That figures!'

Her response drips sardonically from her mouth. She fills the letters in and then takes a big swig of her tea. The old clock on the wall chimes in acknowledgement that time has indeed reached the hour again. It peals away to itself and then falls silent again.

'OK, eleven down, ten letters, the clue is "that which is hard to contain"? The second and third letters are X and C, last letter is T.'

'Excitement!' I shout.

Contempt surrounds her face again.

'Mmm, I just about remember that.'

She begins to fill in the answer whilst speaking the letters aloud,

'E-X-C-I-T-E-M-E-N-T.'

She begins blowing at the answer with her beautiful lips.

'What are you doing?' I ask.

'Blowing the cobwebs off the word; it's been so long since I saw it last. Funny, it doesn't look the same as I remember it.'

That one catches me right between the eyes, but then I am building up resistance now. I have been hit there so many times in the past. I try to persuade her again.

'Come on, leave that now. Go and have a nice shower, put your glad rags on, and we'll go out.'

She rustles the paper in her hands.

'It's too late now, and besides, there's something good on TV later that I want to watch.'

The word 'contrary' must have been created with Ginny in mind. I know the real reason why she doesn't want to go out with me, of course; plain and simple. Because there is no excitement in that anymore, is there? No, that has been undone by one act of foolhardiness; and it was all Ginny's doing.

I admit defeat and decide to take myself out for a walk. I leave her sitting in the darkness watching some nonsense on the television. She is watching some sort of reality show involving five 'C-List' celebrities. They are parachuting out of an aeroplane. Of the five parachutes, only one is working. The remaining four celebrities would have no choice but to fall to certain horrible death. At least that's how I think the game show works. Or is that wishful thinking on my part?

I close the front door behind me and lock it solidly. I double lock the yale lock and put the mortice lock on also. I always like to make sure Ginny is safe and sound if I leave her alone at home. That is why I lock her in with care. I have taken extra measures and put a couple of CCTV cameras in the house. Amazing how easy that was to do and how I can keep an eye on everything from an app on my phone. It helps me ensure Ginny is safe; that she isn't under any threat whilst I am away from home.

I take steps from Grangetown, via Riverside, and into old Temperance Town. The nightlife is in a transitional period. Early revellers are being replaced by lovers of the late show. The dancers, romancers, and seekers of a good time. Ginny always likened it to a shift change. I pass the taxi ranks, protectively lit from above by streetlamps. I carry on wandering the square mile, not knowing exactly where I want to be or where I want to go. This is where it starts, the deep-rooted loneliness awakens and starts to slowly eat at my soul. And it's all her fault; Ginny. If it wasn't for her stupidity, then we could be walking these streets together. We could have been going out for dinner or the movies. I am being unfair to her, though. There were three people involved, three people that allowed this mess to happen, all guilty in their own way. Yes, I blame Ginny for her indiscretions with him, her lover. I blame him for turning the head of a married woman. I blame myself the most for not seeing what was there in front of my eyes until it was far too late.

So, forgiveness is found wanting. It is now a roadblock on the highway of our life together. I can't do it, and Ginny knows that. It doesn't help that I constantly relive the moment when she told me she had given herself to someone else; her words gnaw away at me every day and night. I tell myself it was only once that it happened. However, my head insists there were many more times, many more times he touched and kissed her; and now I hate him.

That's why I come here to Temperance Town. It's here I try and block the damning images of her infidelity I have created from my head. Sometimes all I hear are choirs, the gospel kind. Some nights I imagine Mahalia Jackson singing over the sounds of the buses, cars and trains. I am hearing those choirs again now, but they aren't working. No, the choirs are singing out of tune now. I need to find him, the man who turned Ginny's head. But I don't know where to begin. I look around me as I walk down Wood Street towards St Mary Street. I spy every male face. I could be looking at the bastard now and wouldn't know it. Anger chips away at me again and again.

I walk by the bus station and spot a young couple in a full embrace, the power of love in its infancy. A bag lays at the male's feet as he says his goodbyes to the female. The coach's engine is running, and the door lays open to take him away from her. Their shared sadness penetrates me. What they don't realise is that their longing for each other is at its most intense here and now. I know that much. And once they have parted, that longing will slowly ebb until she knows he is coming back. It may be too late for them by then, of course.
I arrive at the doors of Maddigans and nod at the two guys on the door. They don't know me but recognise me as a regular. One of them holds the door open for me. Once inside, I head to a gap at the bar.

'Pint of Dark and a Spiced Rum please, Roisin.'

She dutifully obliges and places the drinks in front of me.

'How are you doing, Vic?'

'Got a couple of hours to spare?'

'That bad, is it?'

I sip at the glass whilst surveying the people around me. Maybe he is here; maybe that bastard is in this very room. But I'll never know, I guess.

The bar quietens off briefly. I look back to Roisin.

'How're things between you and Ginny?' she asks.

'Not the best. It's just tormenting me so much.'

'No Vic, that's you. You are creating the torment.'

'I got to find him!'

'And what will you do then?'

'I'll rip his fucking lungs out!'

'Not in here you won't. Now stop being so stupid. There's nothing you can do about it. You need to put it to bed.'

'Like he put my Ginny to bed?'

'Soz, but you know what I mean. You don't even know what he looks like, or what his name is.'

'I've asked and asked her. She just shrugs, tells me it'll do no good.'

'She's right too, Vic,' Roisin responds.

'I got something out of her. She says his name was Jimmy.'

'That narrows it down then.'

Roisin shakes her head as she walks away from me. I decide to brood some more.

*****

Ginny sat in the kitchen with a gin and tonic for company. She was enjoying the peace, even though she was being held prisoner. That's what Vic was doing, after all, keeping her away from all temptation. Ginny wasn't that bad, though. She had occasionally spent an evening swiping right on various dating apps in Vic's absence. It was a little bit of harmless escapism. Fidelity had been a struggle for her over the years on more than one occasion. They were always one-night stands.

Ginny blamed her parents for her indiscretions. Both her mother and father had strayed when she was young. She witnessed the fallout, the decay of faithfulness, devotion, and of love itself. The insecurity and absence of a loving family hub left her rudderless until she met Vic. He seemed nice and treated her well. She reciprocated. Believing herself to be in love with him, they married a year after they had met in a nightclub on Charles Street. The weird thing was that she always had trouble remembering the name of the club. She remembered the music, though; Anita Baker and Mary J Blige were her favourites.

Ginny soon realised that marrying Vic was not enough. She didn't know how she felt about him now, they co-existed together, and that was all. They still slept in the same bed, but there was no contact unless Vic's arm drifted across her chest in his sleep. So, she strayed now and then, the thrill of the chase and all that, she supposed. But this last tryst was different; he was younger and fitter. He was funny, and his confidence barely contained itself beneath his skin. Yes, this guy was different. He was 'leaving material'. But it wasn't reciprocated. So, she enjoyed a few dates with the guy, culminating in a night of passion in a Travelodge near the M4. She knew that night would land her in trouble. Ginny knew Vic wasn't going to be overjoyed at her coming home so late but figured it would be worth it. Then, one night as they ate dinner, she told Vic everything. Her food sat untouched on her plate as she stared at it and spoke. Her words fell at a steady pace, the offloading of lies. Her words tore down the wall of trust between them brick by brick. But she only told him of her latest assignation. The past was the past, and there was no point in increasing the pain. She'd said enough. In fact, she could almost hear the moment Vic's heart broke.

Since that night, she didn't go out anymore unless it was with Vic, which was getting less and less now. She often thought about Jimmy, the one that got away. She texted him now and then, but he never answered. In reality, she wasn't that stupid; she knew he had only wanted one thing from her. She gave it to him, and he then moved on to his next conquest. She wasn't sure how she felt about being another notch on a bedpost, mind. She poured another drink, dropping ice cubes into the glass at the same time. Their clinking into the glass was the loudest sound in the house at that moment.

*****

I get thrown to the floor by one of the gorillas. His colleague holds the door open for me as he does so. Admittedly I am a bit pissed and may have stepped out of line. Roisin looks on as gorilla number one barks at me,

'Don't come back, sunshine! You are barred!'

I stand back up. Against my better judgement, I decide to face them up.

'But I didn't do anything!'

Roisin tries to reason with me.

'Vic, you can't go around picking fights with random people! You need to go home and get some rest. This isn't helping you at all.'

'I'm going to find the fucking bastard. He's destroyed me, destroyed my marriage too, he has ... bastard!'

Gorilla number two walks towards me, and I clench my fist as he speaks.

'Look mate, go home. Sober yourself up and I am sure whatever it is will seem better in the morning.'

Gorilla number one spots my clenched fist. He walks towards me.

'I'd move on now if I was you, mate … I mean RIGHT NOW!'

I unclench my hand.

Roisin gently pulls him back. She softens her voice,

'Go home, Vic, please?'

'Sorry, Roisin,' I reply.
I turn and make my way to the taxi rank across the road.

*****

I unlock the Yale lock and mortice locks. I find my way to the kitchen. Ginny is sitting at the table. I notice the redness of her eyes and the packet of tissues on the table.

'Miss me?' I ask.

'No more than usual,' she sniffs back.

'Been anywhere nice?' she asks.

'Just walking.'

She picks the paper back up and looks at the crossword again.

'You didn't finish it then?' I enquire.

'I have one left.'

'Maybe I can help?'

My words are slurred. I am unable to hide my lack of sobriety.

'Maybe you can,' she says with a trace of bitterness. 'Twenty-five across, nine letters, the clue is "pardoning", the first three letters are F-O-R and it ends with a G.'

I know the answer, but I can't say it.

'Any ideas?' she asks.

She knows I know the answer. And I know that she knows too.

'Bloody crossword always beats me!' she moans.

We both trip over that stumbling block once again. Ginny gets up and leaves the kitchen. I follow her and turn the kitchen light off, leaving it in its embracing darkness. I go to the front door and ensure it is locked properly. I remove the key from the keyhole and place it in my pocket for safekeeping. There is only one way I can make sure she won't stray from me again. There is only one way to keep her to myself, to make sure no one else ever touches her again. I turn the passage light out and follow her up the staircase.

Swiping Right

'I'm telling you he was bollock naked!' I say to her. Charly can barely contain her hysterics as I continue my story.

'And I thought *you could have at least waited until we got out of the taxi, you dirty bastard.*'

'You don't half pick them, Mari!' she guffaws.

'I knew it was never going to last, but I shagged him anyway.'

Charly yelps loudly with laughter. I unscrew the top off my hipflask. Charly accepts the vessel from me. The voddie and coke widen her grin as it hits the back of her throat. I reflect on the tale I have just told her. Yes, it was just easy sex, and I'm not proud of it. In fact, the thought leaves me feeling seedy; it's not what I want, of course. Finding the right guy is hard, though. So, I get myself a takeaway now and then; a girl has her needs, after all. Deep down, though, I just want to find the right guy.

The train jolts its way out of Pantycelyn Station. It's late Saturday afternoon, and we are making our way to the big bad city for a night out. It isn't just a night out, though. I may have finally found myself a date online. Desi looks the part on his profile. He states that he is an animal lover. I reckon that's probably a lie for a start, but I still admire the effort and good intentions hidden by his words. He is twenty-eight and lives in Cardiff. He loves Grime, Stormzy and Wiley in particular. His favourite cuisine is Indian, and he is an avid Cardiff City fan. He hates rugby and liars and thinks the idea of eating fish is disgusting. He is a big *Love Island* fan and admits to being a bit of a gym bunny. He seems mostly ideal, and I can always change any bits I'm not keen on, especially his dislike of rugby.

Charly is joining me as my wing-woman. She is here for moral support and to ensure that I don't do anything daft on my first date with this guy. To be fair, I think Charly liked the sound of Desi too, when she read his profile. He is six feet tall, with dark hair - a walking cliché, maybe. I need to watch her, though. She tends to play up to her girlfriend's men. There is no malice intended. She's just a bit of an attention junkie, I guess.

The train trundles between Abercynon and Pontypridd. We have polished off my hipflask and are now tucking into Charly's, which contains Bacardi and coke. Hopefully, it will last the rest of the journey. I check my appearance using my iPhone. Charly stares on down the carriage at her peers, all off to the city for a night of debauchery. She shakes her head from side to side as she watches young men play-fighting and chucking beer over each other.

'Look at those idiots!'

'Just ignore them, Charly.'

'They think women are attracted by that sort of behaviour?'

'We are when we're pissed,' I reason.

'No way, I think I need to look for an older man.'

'One that still has his own teeth, I hope?'

'Anyway, have you heard from this Desi today? You text him a thousand times already, I guess?'

'First thing this morning, and then lunchtime. I sent him a photo of the sandwich I had lunchtime as it goes.'

'Cheese and ham?'

'Yes, as it goes!' I reply.

'What time are we meeting then?'

'Well, I thought me and you would have an hour together first, a bit of Dutch courage, isn't it.'
Charly hands the hipflask back to me.

'You got to watch it, though, Mari. Don't want to get too pissed before you meet him.'
I take a swig and then look away from her.

'I know what I am doing, kiddo. It'll be fine. So, I said we'd meet them in that Maddigans in St Mary Street.'
Charly wriggles in her seat with all the excitement of a child going to the circus.

'I love it there. More to the point, I love those two bouncers on the door!'
I raise my eyes and stare back at her.

'Yeah, they're pretty hot, to be honest.'

'I can think of a far worse backup plan if it all goes tits up tonight.'
We both shriek laughing. The train edges us nearer to the evening.

*****

'You hear about Kylie?' asked Jammo.

'That silly bastard, what's he done now?'

'He's having a tattoo of his dead dog on his leg.'
Desi sucked on his beer bottle as he frowned. He swallowed hard. The sun shone weakly onto them as they sat on a couple of empty beer crates on Desi's mum's front porch.

'His dead dog?!'
Jammo gently flicked the ash off his cigarette into a lone dirty ashtray perched on the garden wall.

'Yep.'

'On his leg?!'

Jammo answered quickly as he raised the contraband back to his mouth.

'That's what he told me.'

Desi shook his head in disgust.

'That's bad!'

'No, I mean a tattoo of his dog, not a tattoo of his dead dog with the tread-marks of the transit van that ran over him!'

'I was gonna say. But then nothing would surprise me with him.'

The front of Desi's mum's house resembled a forgotten building site. It was as if the builders left early one Friday afternoon some months before and never came back. The concrete driveway hosted an overflowing skip. There were planks on what little grass grew in the front garden. Ladders and scaffold poles lay on the path at the side of the house. The gates hung loosely off decaying hinges at the entrance to the drive. Paint peeled itself slowly off the wrought iron.

Jammo removed his Stussy baseball cap and ran his fingers through his curly auburn hair. His sallow complexion was waving goodbye to the acne of his teenage years, but it was taking its time. Jammo's top lip held onto a wispy moustache. His blues eyes homed in on Desi. He wanted nothing more than to be him; simple as. A smile struck him across the mouth.

'What's so funny?' asked Desi.

'Nothing.'

Desi stretched out his skinny-jeaned long legs and pushed his back to the wall. He briefly squinted at the sky. His long angular nose defined his sharp jawline. Both guys picked up their beers in unison. If only synchronised swigging was an Olympic event. Jammo couldn't help himself; his grin grew wider than the Bristol Channel.

'Never thought I'd see the day, mind.'
'See what day exactly?'
''Today, this day, tonight, you, internet dating, swiping right, dodgy profiles. Animal lover, for fuck's sake! Really?'
'Everyone's doing it,' Desi defended.
'I'm not doing it!" taunted Jammo.
'No, but your mum is, I hear.'
'Can you blame her after that last prick she was seeing? Anyway, I thought you were seeing that Cindy from the chippy?'
'Nah, I caught her sucking off Dibby behind the Cons Club.'
'Dibby?!'
'Yeah.'
'Dibby Edwards?'
'Yeah.'
'He's your cousin, ain't he?'
'Cousin removed now!'

Jammo shook his head disapprovingly, and silence grew between them. It was shattered by Desi lobbing his empty bottle into the rubbish skip.

'One-nil!' he teased.

Jammo smiled again.

'To be honest, my mum has met a couple of nice guys online.'
'She deserves it, mate. She's still a looker.'
'Leave it out, will you?'
'I tell you now, I would!'

Jammo grabbed Desi around the neck with a playful yet firm squeeze and released him with a frisky push. He finished his bottle and repeated Desi's shot into the skip. Desi created a light ripple of mock applause. Reaching for two fresh bottles of beer, he uncapped them on the brick wall.

'Anyway, talking of Kylie, have you sorted any gear for tonight? We need to be on top form for meeting these two young ladies.'

'It's safe and proper, Bro.'

*****

The lane was normally quiet on a Saturday evening. People were either tearing it up in town or maybe just nipping down to Canton for a bit of drunken carnage. Eddie sat behind the wheel of the slow-moving car, Sheri at his side. They knew there wouldn't be much in the way of action, but they didn't care. Things would no doubt get busier later in the evening. They would both be supporting the late shift in town then. That would be a totally different beast to manage. So now was for having a little drive around, a little quiet time. Sheri adjusted her shades from the sun as it sat low in the sky.

'This is fun, isn't it, Eddie?'

He grinned as he gently took the corner from the lane onto Cowbridge Road West. Sheri was different from his last partner, Jeff. He was a stickler for authority. No bad thing, of course. Jeff considered himself a peacemaker, a total devotee of law and order, to protect and serve and all that. Sheri didn't take things quite so seriously. She made Eddie laugh; in fact, he hadn't laughed so much since they started working together.

'Hate the Saturday night shift, though, Eddie? Don't you?'

'How long have we been working together now?' he asked.

'About six months, I think.'

'And how many times in that six months have you asked me that question?'

'Dunno. More than once, I suppose?'

They both laughed. His heartstrings tightened; they were ready to be strummed. He couldn't do or say anything, though; he had to stay professional. Besides, what would his wife Eleri think; even if she had passed away five years since? Either way, Sheri had shown him he could laugh again. Her blonde curly hair was always tied up with perfection. She had cheeky dimples and the cutest of noses. Her smile could light up a stormy valley at night, and he was falling for her. She never had a clue; at least, that's what he thought. He knew she was single again after breaking up with that idiot Wayne. That man knew nothing about women. He knew nothing about showing them respect, kindness, and love.

Sometimes Eddie wished they could just drive around together all day undisturbed. Maybe he'd chuck a picnic hamper in the boot, and they could drive off to Ogmore beach for the day. He'd put a blanket on the ground, and they could lay back and listen to the sea. But then again, it might not be practical. What would the public think for a start? The sight of two police officers kissing on a blanket in the daylight would be inconceivable. *That wouldn't look too good to the Chief-Super*, he thought to himself. So, it was to be a secret that he would carry with him forever, Sheri and her smile as big as the sky. *Everyone had a secret love, after all,* Eddie figured. That thought carried some comfort for him.

He took the car to the roundabout at Culverhouse Cross. Eddie then doubled back before slipping right off Cowbridge Road West onto Heol Trelai.

'What are we doing up this neck of the woods anyway, Eddie?'

'Just looking.'

'For?'

'Coppers are always looking, Sheri. We're always sniffing out the bad guys.'

'Why here, though?'

'It's as good as anywhere. Remember, bad guys don't differentiate between here, Cyncoed, or Timbuktu. Bad guys are everywhere, and we're going to get them.'

She smiled back.

'Listen to Dirty Harry!'

They headed back onto the lane and drove its length back to the lights at the junction of Cowbridge Road West. As they pulled up to the red light, Eddie spotted a fracas in the bus shelter on the other side of the road. Four men were grappling with each other and shouting. Eddie jumped the lights and pulled up at the kerbside.

Two of the men ran off. Eddie shouted for them to stop; it was pointless, of course. White powder and a broken plastic bag sat on the pavement. Some of the powder lay on the top of Desi and Jammo's highly polished shoes.

Jammo raised his hands,

'It ain't what it looks like, man!'

Desi whispered obscenities at the sky as he clasped his head in his hands.

Sheri wasted no time slapping the cuffs on Jammo.

Eddie pulled out the cuffs for Desi.

'Don't tell me. You're both off to a cookery lesson, and that's the self-raising flour on the floor?'

Desi offered out his wrists.

'Yeah, and it's gluten-free.'

Sheri began to read them both their rights. Eddie reported the two fleeing assailants on his radio. He was confident he would be seeing them again.

****

Mari narrowly missed being late on duty. The sun illuminated the early Sunday afternoon sky. She almost missed the last train home the night before. Desi didn't show up for their date either. She chastised herself for being stupid enough to believe he would; it wasn't the first time this had happened. Charly got lucky, though. She met a guy called Wayne. They were all over each other like cheap coats. He had one of those familiar faces, but Mari couldn't fathom it out. Her mood had deflated throughout the evening, like a car tyre with a very slow puncture.

Desi had made her look and feel a fool. Charly did her bit to keep Mari's spirits going. Mari mistakenly thought he might be a good prospect. She hoped she would have the chance to discover some semblance of romance and, eventually, love. She was pretty upset when she got home. Her mum was still up waiting for her. She could see Mari was unhappy about something, but she was no use in these situations; she offered no succour in such circumstances. She never understood the online thing, and why should she? Mari always told her that was the modern way. That was how people met. But she wasn't so sure now.

The night had the potential for total misery after Desi didn't show. Charly was up for anything, though, and Mari did roar laughing when she danced up to a man at the bar. She was singing 'Don't You Want Me Baby?' like Shirley Bassey through a megaphone. The man walked away laughing. It took brute strength to get her out of Wayne's clutches later, though. Still, they had a train to catch; there was no way Mari was paying for a frigging taxi. She managed to prise them apart at the entrance to Maddigans. The two bouncers laughed at her attempts to drag Charly away. Mari watched her exchange numbers with her newfound love, and then they legged it to the station. It had been an eventful evening for all the wrong reasons.

That was then, though, and this was now. Mari headed off to check in with the desk sergeant. She stood back briefly as she watched him charging a tall young man with dark hair for possession of Class A drugs. The man shrugged as the charges were read out. It was then she recognised him; the man she first saw when she was swiping right.

'Desi?'

God's Empty Chair

'That's total bollocks!'
Spanish Ianto's face reddened as he spat out his beer-soaked words. Shoni Patel smiled at Ianto's fearless outburst. He admired his bravado and his derring-do. Truth be told, Shoni loved Spanish Ianto, however opinionated the man was.
Harri Spoons wasn't to be browbeaten by Ianto's retort, though.

'I'm telling you, league is far better than union!'
Dai Scissors thought it a good moment to interject. He felt it his mission to take the heat out of the exchange.

'I think Harri has a point, Ianto, it's faster for a start.'
Spanish Ianto leant forward and stared him down from his bar stool.

'Who rattled your bastard cage, Vidal Sassoon!?'
Never had there been more typical Saturday night banter at the Frantic Fox. The small band of men sat awkwardly in a scattered gathering. They were picking holes in each other's thoughts and theories. Spanish Ianto was the most vociferous; he was certainly the most prejudiced. His face was seldom caught with a smile, but then he had nothing to smile about. Life had taken care of that for him. Life does that generally. Taking redundancy from the Splott steelworks at fifty-five years old, he thought he had it made. Yet, as he developed a thriving alcohol problem, so did his small fortune diminish. A messy divorce accompanied Ianto's thriving drinking career. He had a grown-up son he saw on rare occasions and that was it. Things couldn't be any more dysfunctional. So here he was, ten years later, holding court on a well-worn bar stool. His grizzled, reddened face was home to his large, crooked nose.

His eyes carried more bags than the hold of a jumbo jet. His fair hair sat proud and greasy atop his road-worn face.
Maeve placed a tray on the bar. It carried four pints of SA and an orange juice. Her pretty face became long and pointed.

'I'll not tell you lot again. Keep it down. This isn't your living room, and you're upsetting the rest of my clientele!'

The men looked around at a mainly empty bar.
Ianto coughed heartily, his thirty-a-day habit clearly not worrying him.

'Yeah, I can see you've had a bit of a rush on, Maeve.'

Clad in a short black dress, she gripped her hips firmly. Her earrings rattled gently as she speedily threw some words back at him.

'I should bar the lot of you, especially you Ianto, and as for you, Shoni Patel!'

Shoni stared back in disbelief.

'What have I done?'

Maeve was moving up a gear, her tongue hitting the accelerator. She flicked her strawberry blonde hair back from her shoulders with a shake of her head.

'You come in here every night of the week. You prop yourself up at the end of the bar, and all you buy is two orange juices, every frigging night. I'm trying to run a business here! The very sight of you lot puts the punters right off. Doesn't do much for me either, truth be told!'

It was true of Shoni, of course. He never drank alcohol; he was pretty much too scared to. But he wanted to be part of something. He wanted to belong, and it was among this stagnant and almost moribund band of men that he found himself at home. He would arrive every night in his black blazer, blue shirt and red, white, and green striped tie. His grey slacks were fastened at the waist with a frayed purple snake belt. Black patent leather shoes adorned his tiny feet. He would stand and listen to the group's pointless discussions as he sipped at his orange juice. His beard and pitted face sat with intensity under his black turban. Harri Spoons took his fresh beer from the tray and walked back to his chair.

'I don't know why we come here in the first place, in all honesty, Maeve. The table service has declined terribly for a start.'

Maeve let her smile take over from her anger.

'I give up, I really do!'

'You love us, Maeve, even that grumpy twat Ianto over there.'

Maeve walked away from the group, waving her hand in the air whilst her other gripped her hip.

'Bunch of sad bastards, the lot of you!'

Harri felt pleased with himself knowing his words had sent Maeve on her way. He was the enigma of the group. No one knew what he did for a living. They were clueless about how he filled his day. No one knew if he was married, divorced, or living in a tent in Pontcanna fields. He would sit every night in a manky brown leather armchair which sat in the corner, opposite the bar. Much like him, the chair carried a few scars and rips. His tanned bald head held a pair of pebble glasses across his nose. He sat with a plastic majesty in his navy-blue Sergio Tacchini tracksuit. White Reebok trainers adorned his feet. A thick gold rope chain hung vulgarly around his neck. His delusions remained unchecked. This led him to believe he was the leader of this errant pack of drunken self-serving savants.

Sais Johnny sat amongst them on a small wooden stool with his back to the side of the fruit machine. He liked to regard himself as the thinker of the group; in reality, he was more the agent provocateur. His raven hair and handsomely forged and tanned looks gave him the edge of a mysterious gypsy. Sais Johnny always wore black jeans, black shirt, and Cuban heel boots. He topped it all off with a three-quarter-length black leather coat. Bad guys always wore black, and that was him, a bad guy. He sat checking his football bets on his phone. Despite being a man of few words, Sais Johnny loved to lob grenades into a conversation. He would then sit back and watch the fallout. He had proudly started the league versus union debate earlier. Boredom was getting the better of him on that one now, so he thought he'd change the subject.

'Did you hear that they are thinking of removing religion from the curriculum in some schools?'

That was enough. He'd pulled the pin.

'Bloody good idea!' exclaimed Harri Spoons.

Shoni interjected.

'No, no, no, this cannot be. We must respect all religious aspects. Especially when it comes to the education of our children, whatever our beliefs!'

'There ain't no God. It's all a load of tosh,' whined Dai Scissors.

Dai Scissors, indeed, a willowy character who owned a barbershop off Clifton Street in Splott. He liked to join in and give the pretence that he was one of the gang. The truth was that he was regarded by the others as the quiet one. A bit like George Harrison in The Beatles, they joked. He delivered supposedly angered opinions and retorts with such feeble emotion. It didn't stop him from leaning his five-foot skinny frame against the bar next to Spanish Ianto, though. His short-cropped greying haircut some contrast against Ianto's lank and greasy mop.

Ianto slurped at his beer and slammed it back on the bar. Turning to Dai Scissors, he gurned in disbelief.

'Of course, there's a fucking God! Am I surrounded by heathens!?'

'I'm no heathen, Ianto. I'm with you on this,' begged Shoni.

'Don't be so stupid, Shoni. Yes, we may both believe, but you're on a different bus to me on this one. And if you ask me, your driver has lost his fucking way, son!'

Bewildered at Ianto's comments, Shoni stepped back from the debate.

It was Dai's turn to get the Ianto death stare.

'Listen to you. You spout more hot air than comes out of your hairdryer! None of us is exempt. I promise you, come your judgement day, you will find yourself in the chair!'

'What fucking chair?' enquired Harri Spoons.

'God, you lot know nothing! I'm telling you, there won't be no St Peter stood at any gate. No bloke is standing there wielding a clipboard and pen with a list of the latest arrivals. That's all bullshit!'

Harri laughed, Sais Johnny giggled into his phone as he checked his bets again.

Ianto continued.

'When you get there, you'll find yourself in a big room, and it's there that God will face you. It's there that you face the final interview. It's there that he decides if it's heaven or the deepest depths of hell that you will spend in eternity. St Peter? He's a glorified doorman like those two pricks at Maddigans down the road.'

Harri wanted more. He wasn't convinced yet.

'So, you're saying there's a chair in front of God, and he asks you to sit in it whilst he grills you?'

'Yeah, God's Empty Chair it's called.'

'What type of chair?' asked Harri sarcastically,

'I mean, is it an armchair? Or a fucking deckchair?'

'Probably an electric chair,' muttered Sais Johnny.

Dai backed Harri up.

'Yeah, is it a Lazyboy? And how do you know this anyway!?'

'I just know it. It's an uncomfortable chair, and we'll all sit our sorry arses in it one day. Yes, we all end up in God's Empty Chair for the final interview.'

'Does he ask where you see yourself in five years?' joked Dai Scissors.

'Or what your strengths and weaknesses are?' joked Harri Spoons.

Dai laughed.

'I guess being brown bread is pretty much a major weakness!'

Ianto sighed heavily.

'I don't know why I come in here sometimes.'

'It's for the scintillating conversation,' teased Harri.

'You come in here 'cos you are too old to go anywhere else in town,' chipped in Dai Scissors.

'Except Maddigans, of course.' Harri added.

Sais Johnny laughed. Dai continued,

'Yeah, even my grannie drinks in Maddigans!'

'Your grannie's been dead for years!' Ianto retorted.

'That's as maybe, but I think you're missing the point, Ianto,' reasoned Dai.

'She would have sat in the chair when she went,' said Ianto.

Dai's brow furled up,

'Would she now?'

'Yeah, God would have given her a going over, no doubt.'

Maeve had been listening intently to their drunken ramblings.

'And what makes you lot think God is a man?' she chided.

Sais Johnny was feeling pleased with himself now. What started as a religious debate was now becoming a sexist one too. His night was starting to come alive, as was his ACCA bet. Dai Scissors grew uncomfortable.

'That's true, point taken. Sorry, Maeve.'

Ianto turned back from Dai.

'Another round of drinks, Maeve, love, there's a good girl.'

Maeve scowled back at him.

'You familiar with the word misogynist?'

'That's someone good at making cocktails, innit?' teased Harri.

Ianto shrugged his shoulders.

'And a packet of dry roast whilst you're there.'

Maeve drew the pump back angrily as the fluid spilt into the almost clean glass. Rising from his stool, Sais Johnny drew a large breath.

'Now there's a subject, death. Something we all have in common.'

The group went quiet as he continued,

'I'm off for a piss.'

They all looked at each other in his absence. Harri sniggered as Johnny left the room.

'Sometimes I think he is death, dressed in black all the time, like the fucking grim reaper he is.'

The room fell silent for a couple of minutes as Maeve slammed the drinks on the bar. Shoni swilled his orange juice around his glass and decided to risk talking again.

'We all fear it. We all fear that day,' he solemnly muttered.

Johnny walked back into the room as Shoni finished his sentence.

'No, we don't. Our fear lays in when that day will be.'

Ianto ordered whisky chasers for the group. The solemnity of the debate warranted his order. Shoni got a soda water chaser. Johnny sat back on his stool and continued his address.

'There isn't one person here who won't wake up one day and wonder how long they have left. That's where the fear lies. You will have that thought one day … if you haven't already.'

'Morbid bastard!' shouted Harri.

Ianto nodded his approval at Harri's riposte. Dai Scissors shuddered to himself; he then pulled a harmonica out of his pocket. He raised the instrument to his lips. Blowing and sucking, the notes of 'Old Man River' rang out from it. The group laughed loudly among themselves. Spanish Ianto coughed and laughed so hard. His face grew redder, and tears of laughter streamed down his face. He then fell backwards off his stool. Their integrated laughter turned the room's volume up several notches. Ianto lay unconscious on the sticky tiled floor. The laughter quickly subsided. Staring down at Ianto, Shoni let his glass slip between his fingers. The breaking glass threw shards over Ianto's face.

Frankie and the Wonderwall Kid

The pound coin bounces out of my pork pie hat onto the pavement. I nod my thanks to the passer-by as I continue singing. I am about to hit the last chords of Neil Young's 'Heart of Gold'. Placing the pound coin into my hat, I do a quick count-up of its contents. About twenty quid, I reckon. Not bad for this early on a Saturday night. I take a swig from the water bottle at my feet. A couple of girls approach me.

'You know "Brown Eyed Girl", presh?' one asks.

I smile and hit the opening chords. They do a brief little dance. One of them throws a couple of coins into my hat. They sashay up the street laughing and giggling, satisfied customers.

I have brought Chester with me tonight. Normally I leave him at home, but it's Saturday, and he deserves a night out. He dozes on his tartan blanket at my feet as I continue my repertoire. He's the only constant in my life now; truly man's very best friend. I'm on automatic pilot most nights and tonight's no different. I monitor my thoughts as I play on through. The night trade passes me by, all of them moving on. I envy them. I wish I could do the same. But every night is the same now.

I still hope to see her face pop out from the passers-by. Oh, for that moment to happen. I've played it out in my mind so many times. My poor guitar would hit the ground, and I'd run to her. She'd shout my name and envelop me. I'd hold and squeeze her for dear life, and I'd never let her go again. It's not to be, of course, but it doesn't stop me from looking or wishing.

It gets harder when people ask me to play that song too. You know the one. I can't bear to say the title because it's burned into my mind. It's like it's been branded there for life.

If I get a request for it (which happens about a dozen times a night!) I jokingly direct them to another busker down the road called Noel. He doesn't exist, of course. It's just my bit of fun. It was our song, mine and hers. This was because it was the only song I managed to teach her to play on the guitar. The times we'd laugh as I placed her fingers on the fretboard, both of us drunk on red wine. She knew her chords but had never put them to use. So, I decided to try and teach her how to play it. And now I hated it.

I am shaken by a strange request from a lady on a mobility scooter. She is wearing a purple velour tracksuit, brown UGG boots and a blue gilet. She also wears a badge that says, 'I am fifty' and another beneath it with her name on. Her short, bouffant grey hair demands attention.

'You know any Flanagan and Allen, love?' she asks.
I nod and shout,

'Happy 50th birthday, Eileen!'
My rendition of 'Underneath the Arches' has her dancing and singing in her seat. As the song unfolds, I think of my one-time friend Billy Rose who first taught me the song. It was in a similar situation. Billy Rose and I were playing in a pub many years back. Just me and him and a few stragglers at the bar. Our acoustic guitars intertwined as we concluded Pink Floyd's 'Wish You Were Here'. We both reached down for our beers respectively, when a voice chirped from the bar,

'You know any Flanagan and Allen boys?'
I remember recoiling in horror and looking at Billy Rose. I was lost. He smiled back at me and started singing and playing. I studied his chord shapes and repeated them on my guitar. I never forgot the tune after that night. We never got asked to play it again as it goes. That was until tonight. I think of Billy Rose as I sing. He had gone too, like her. I look at the passing crowd, still moving on.

Kylie emerges from the passing crowd. His arrival gives me the opportunity for a break. He's in his late twenties and, as per the cliché, a lovable rogue. He hasn't always been that way, but his mum and dad's divorce sent him south of the law. I first met him back in the day when I was gigging around Cardiff with a few local bands. Kylie is the oracle when it comes to music. His lank blonde hair pokes out from beneath his Burberry cap. His dilated green eyes suggest he's been at the disco biscuits. He shuffles from foot to foot.

'How's your tattoo?' I ask.

'How do you know about that?'

'Jungle drums my friend, how's business?'

'Not good, man. I'm getting rid of what I'm carrying and heading home.'

''Trouble?'

'Feds are cracking down. Can't you feel the heat out here tonight?'

'I'm a fucking busker, and you are a second-division dealer. Not Pablo Escobar!'

He slips me a grin.

'Anything you need?' he asks.

'Yeah, a Land Rover, Kylie. Can you get me one of those?'

'In what colour?' he replies.

I get the feeling he isn't joking.

'Anyway, I gotta get on before Sun Hill turn up.'

I watch him scoot off into the night.

I strike up the chords of 'Bitter Sweet Symphony'. A couple raise their thumbs in approval as they walk by. I think of her again. I wonder if H. G. Wells ever did invent that machine.

*****

I first met Billy Rose in the very early nineties. I'd been on a wander one night, and as I passed the Claude pub, I heard a screaming guitar solo coming from the building. There was an A4 poster in the window announcing the band. 'Monkeyhouse' seemed a funny name, but I was intrigued enough to enter. As I did so, the song came to an explosive climax. Crashing cymbals cut across a sonic battleground. The guitarist chucked his wine-red Gibson Les Paul Custom into its stand. He then stumbled off the stage. His long blonde locks straddled his lean shoulders as he pushed his way to the bar. He wore a sweaty Jack Daniel's t-shirt and ripped jeans. A pair of battered Converse finished the ensemble. I stood with my back to the bar. He stood next to me and ordered a Wild Turkey.

'Nice guitar,' I offered.

The guitarist shrugged,

'Fucker never stays in tune!'

Whilst I was no Leo Fender or Les Paul, I knew a bit about guitars.

'That's expensive guitars for you!' I chuckled nervously.

'It hasn't been right since I stuck it over some guy's head at a gig across the water a few years back.'

'Really?!' I gulped.

'You know 5:15 by The Who?'

'Out of my brain on the train!' I sang back at him.

'That's the one; well, the fucker had the temerity to tell me what key I should play it in!'

With that, the guitarist reached out his hand to me. This was Billy Rose.

We became good friends as time elapsed, often going to see other bands together. I followed Monkeyhouse around and witnessed some excellent and not-so-excellent gigs. I revealed to him that I also played the guitar. Then one night at the Inn on the River, he called me up to join in the encore. It was a terrifying yet liberating moment for me.

It wasn't long after that he asked me to join the band. It was a dream moment. We played across the valleys, we played around most of south and west Wales, come to that. We occasionally crossed the river into England too. I loved those gigs in particular; they made me feel like a proper musician touring the land. And then came the day I met her.

I was spending an evening at the Chapter Arts Centre. There was a band called Bijoux Too treading the boards. Their sparkly guitar pop filled the room. I spied my dream girl, Frankie, leaning against the end of the bar with a bottle of Newcastle Brown in her hand. She was alone. I noticed her scarlet red fingernails as she clasped the drink. I remember thinking that she looked like Chrissie Hynde. She had the darkest hair, and her blue eyes were set deep with mascara. Her lips were those of a Spanish dancer. She was gently pouting, sultriness personified. She also looked like dangerous fun in leather pants. Her heels added six inches to her stature. I had to overcome any feelings of intimidation if I was to get to know her. I needn't have worried; she took the battle to me instead. She walked toward me slowly, my breathing stopped for a few seconds, and my pulse started to sprint away. She kissed my cheek; her voice was pure velvet.

'I know you.'

I gulped again,

'Really?'

'You play the guitar. I know, I've seen you.'

'I do my bit,' I replied with false nonchalance.

I tried to play up to her recognition, but I was wasting my time.

'I play too,' she informed me,

'but I'm not as good as you.'

I laughed and then nodded toward the band as they played.

'What do you think?'

'Not my thing, to be honest. That's not to say they aren't good, of course. To be truthful, I need some air.'

She winked at me as she left the bar. I was captivated as I followed her out.

We became inseparable after that meeting, and it wasn't long before Frankie moved in with me. She brought a holdall full of clothes and a pink case full of vinyl records with her. A leopard skin make-up case and a low-budget Fender acoustic guitar moved in too. The back of the guitar had a Beatles sticker accompanied by a Joni Mitchell one.

Every day was electric. Every night was the same, times two. She breathed life into me. She made me realise how much I was missing from life. Frankie didn't want anything to be boring. She wanted every breathing moment to be a new thrill, a new thing learned, a new experience for each new day. I was mesmerised and had never known a woman quite like her. We traded chords and tunes. She was getting better and starting to form her own little repertoire of songs. She referred to me as her 'master' when it came to learning new tunes. She became my acolyte, my disciple, even.

Then came the day that we heard that song for the first time. Frankie picked up the words immediately. I worked out the chords and dug out my Capo, and that was it. We would sing it a dozen times a night, before bedtime, when in bed, and again in the morning. It was our tune, and there was no disputing it. The Chinese guy in the flat below us loved it too. He'd bang his ceiling in time with it. It was obvious he liked it. Eventually, the landlord turned up to chastise me for the noise. I remember his words as he left.

'I don't need the bloody neighbours coming to me complaining about the Wonderwall kid! You got it?!'

Frankie laughed as he stormed out of the flat, and that was it; the name stuck. Despite this little incident, life was simply bliss. And then I truly screwed things up.

My knee got very sore the night I asked Frankie to marry me. We stood by the fountains outside the City Hall. I was convinced the time was right. I looked up at the stars to check their alignment. Frankie just stared down at me as I finished my words. She said nothing as my heart spun around like a thousand fans. My knee cramped up, and I tumbled forward. Frankie helped me up, and we traversed to a bench. Sitting gently, I rubbed at my knee.

'That went well,' I joked aloud.

She held back her tears as she spoke.

'It's not for me. It's certainly not for us.'

I looked up again. Obviously, one or two stars were off course tonight.

'Why? I love you, Frankie, and I know you love me.'

'I do, but I can't do the marriage thing. I know what it does to people. I don't think I could stand the tedium and boredom that being married would bring.'

'But it won't!'

I was starting to sound desperate.

'I promise you, Frankie, things won't change.'

'In time they will, though, and I don't want that. I don't want to be stifled and resentful. I need to be free to make my own choices. I don't need any ball and chain!'

Her last words were dripped in anger, and she knew it. Then she uttered the last two words I ever heard her speak.

'I'm sorry.'

Frankie kissed me gently and then got up from the bench. It was then she walked away, never to be seen again.

A few days later, Billy Rose called me with some new gig dates. But I wasn't interested. He sensed something wrong on the call. I quit there and then. I was never to play with Monkeyhouse again. The band strangely disappeared from the scene after that. But I couldn't have cared less.

*****

I decide to finish the night early by denying a request from another intoxicated passer-by. A drunken woman asks me for 'Shape of You' as she clings to her less drunk male accomplice. Given my dislike of the ginger busker, I redirect her to another fictitious busker down the road.

'I don't know it, unfortunately, but there's a fellow busker in Mill Lane who'll do it for you. His name is Ned Beercan,' I joke.

I pack up and wander off down Chip Alley. Chester follows behind. I get chips and curry sauce and sit down on the pavement to devour them. Chester gets excited as I chuck him a couple of chips. I see Kylie again as he runs past me towards St Mary Street. I smile at him, but he looks like trouble is chasing him down again.

'Can't stop, man. I gotta get out of here!'

The problem with Kylie is that he'll never learn. I know this and have told him countless times. My advice always washes over him, though. I wonder why I bother or care.

An hour later, I am home. I am dropping the needle into the groove. I love vinyl, and tonight's choice is The Stones' 'Exile on Main Street'. She loved this album, as did Billy Rose. The one thing that reminds me of them both. I light a cigarette and smile to myself. Blowing smoke into the air, I think of the Difford and Tilbrook song, 'Cigarette of a Single Man'. I make a mental note to play it later. 'Rocks Off' rips out from the speakers via the vinyl. I sit back and wonder to myself where Billy Rose and Frankie are now. I switch my attention back to the music. I know it's proper music, not the populist shite I play on the streets every night. I feel like a musical whore at times, like I prostitute myself on the streets as I play music I mostly hate. But I have to eat, I have to keep Chester fed, and I have rent to pay. I think of Billy Rose and Frankie again. I turn the music up louder; the Chinese man below bangs on the ceiling again.

The Cooler's Tale

Brad felt like a freight train was running through his chest. His heart pounded at great speed as he stepped out of the shower. Wrapping the grey towel around him, he checked his face in the mirror. His skin remained smooth, but his eyes bore dark circles. It added to his broodiness. He could feel the chest palpitations. He knew they would be subsiding soon, but it didn't lessen the dread. His good friend, anxiety, raced through his body. He held onto the white enamel wash basin and tapped a couple of his fingers furiously on it. He took deep breaths and told himself it was going to pass. His head lightened, and he felt faint for a moment.

His doctor had told him they were panic attacks. Brad thought the medicine man was full of shit but accepted his prognosis in time. It made sense when he thought about it, of course. His attacks had started two weeks after that night; the night he was badly beaten up in a nightclub. Violence accompanied his work, and he had no problem dealing with it until that night. It had taken him some time to get over it and return to work. He had turned down counselling, naturally. The thought of discussing his feelings with anyone else was alien to him. Men didn't do that sort of thing anyway, did they? But, like it or not, the effect that night had on him left so many scars, most of them mental.

Angie left him a while after it happened. She pleaded for him to give the job up and do something else. He point-blank refused, and things between them fell apart. They both drifted into a world without communication. It eventually became a world without love. That hurt him, but life went on regardless. He was single now and not particularly ready to mingle. He didn't think he'd be ready anytime soon, either.

Two of his attackers got sent down for two years each. The third assailant got ten years for attempted murder. Brad was in court when they all got sentenced. It didn't help him, though; the night terrors and panic remained.

The panic attack had now subsided, and Brad took to getting himself ready for work. He sat at his kitchen table, readying himself for another night of keeping the peace. He didn't look forward to the vomiting idiots and roid heads, the jealous boys and girls. It was what Angie had once called the underbelly of decaying humanity. What else was he going to do, though? He could only hope it would be a quiet night. He slugged back the shot of whisky and sat the dirty glass in the washing-up bowl, just another drop of Dutch courage.

*****

Roisin dabbed the cream on Tony's back. The wound was well healed now but, being the narcissist he was, he wanted to make sure the scar looked as good as it could. She winced as she rubbed the cream in gently. However much it had healed, she was still afraid of hurting him as she applied the balm.

'It's looking good, lovely boy,' she encouraged.

'I hate asking you to do this, but I don't have anyone else,' he responded.

'Not a problem. It's my pleasure, treasure.'

There wasn't much room available for the pair of them in the back office at Maddigans. Whilst Roisin felt slightly awkward in this situation, she knew Tony wouldn't try anything on. Besides, she'd kick him in the balls if he did.

'That bastard should have got life for doing that to you!'

'It's done now. No point in getting wound up about it. Besides, all the birds love a scar.'

She gently clipped him across his head,

'Birds?!'

He laughed. Tony secretly loved the attention he was getting from her. He warmed to her gentle strokes as she rubbed the lotion into his wound. She had no idea at all about how he felt about her. She had everything he sought in a woman. She was funny, smart, and gentle. To put it simply, he loved her. But he had never told her. No, he'd just keep that little nugget to himself. She'd never go for him, of course. He was too much of a bloke, although he often thought it might be an idea to tap into his feminine side. But he couldn't see himself expressing his emotions and feelings or wearing a man bag anytime soon.

He buttoned his shirt up and tucked it back in once she was finished. As he turned to face her, she planted a little kiss on his forehead.

'Go get 'em, Floyd!' she teased.

*****

It was true; I did love Roisin. But I couldn't do much about it. She wasn't aware of it, and the management frowned upon staff getting involved with each other. I say she wasn't aware of it, but maybe she was. She often smiled at me, but there again, she often smiled at everyone. No, Roisin was strictly off-limits to me. But you can't help who you fall in love with. I just had to get on with my job. I don't think Brad knew about my unspoken love.

Thing is, with me and Brad, we're just blokes, aren't we? We're basic, what some people would call 'meat and potatoes' type of guys. It goes with the job. We're deemed as nothing more than meatheads. But we're not. We need to be good negotiators, arbitrators, and counsellors even. But people don't see that, especially when they are steaming drunk. What runs concurrently with this is that we can have the pick of the women and that we are promiscuous. That viewpoint isn't entirely wrong, but it's not for me, and I am sure Brad is the same. Having said all that, some things are definitely off the agenda for two blokes like us. One of those things is talking about love. Much as I loved Brad, I wouldn't have discussed anything like this with him. Well, men don't, do they? That's just how we are. There was nothing I wouldn't do for Brad; I even saved his life once. But I wouldn't tell him about this, no way.

I hated watching guys chat Roisin up whilst she worked. I felt a little stab of pain in my gut when I saw that happen. It was lucky I spent a lot of my time outside the door. But who was I to do anything about it? She was a free agent at the end of the day. I knew one or two guys from her past too. One of them was a right waster. He still is as it goes. She was well rid of him. He still showed up at the club, though, normally when he was in trouble, which was most of the time. I just wanted her to be happy at the end of the day, I guess. But it would never be with me.

*****

Kylie stood in front of Tony and Brad at the entrance to Maddigans. His lank blonde hair was still poking out from beneath his Burberry cap. Beads of sweat ran down his forehead.

'You're kidding, right?' asked Tony.

Brad manifested his edginess by shuffling from foot to foot.

'Come on, man, I need to see her for a second,' Kylie pleaded.

'Why?! So, you can sponge some money off her?'

'I just need to see her.'

Brad checked out his dilated eyes.

'What you on, Kylie?'

Kylie pulled out a small bag of pills from his pocket.

'Look, you can have a couple of phets if you let me in – on the house.'

Tony took a step forward and grabbed him by the collar.

'Have you lost your fucking mind, sunshine!?'

'Please, mate, I am begging you!'

'What do you reckon, Brad, this Herbert reckons he's begging us?'

'I don't see him on his knees, though, Tony? I don't think he's trying hard enough if you ask me,' Brad teased.

Kylie began to sweat harder; Tony tightened his grip. Suddenly there was a crash from across the road. A man had thrown a traffic cone at another man as they fought in the street. Tony released Kylie and ran into the road. Brad shook his head and then followed him. Kylie took his chance and darted into the bar.

*****

'I'm busy, Kylie. What do you want?'

He looked at her sheepishly. It was a look she had seen a million times. He fidgeted with a beer mat.

She folded her arms closely into her chest as she scrutinised him.

'Let me guess. You want money?'

'I'm in the shit, Roisin. I need five hundred quid.'

'Five hundred?!! What the hell for? And what makes you think I have that kind of money!?'

'You don't want to know.'

She poured him a half pint of lager.

'Sorry, but you got no chance. That's on the house, and it's all you are getting!'

Kylie lifted the glass from the bar.

'Desi and Jammo got lifted by the feds earlier.'

Roisin shook her head in disgust.

'I couldn't give a shit about those two idiots.'

'They bought some dust from me earlier, and I don't trust that Jammo. I reckon he'll grass. That's why I need the money. I got to get away from here for a bit!'

'You idiot, you're still dealing? God, I had a very lucky escape when I kicked your arse out the door, didn't I!?'

'You loved me once, Roisin.'

'Yeah, I probably did,' she sighed.

'Well, you won't be getting any cash from me, unfortunately. Now drink up El Chapo and do one. I don't want any shit happening here because of you.'

Kylie drained his glass as Tony and Brad poked their heads through the door. Tony's face reddened as he spotted him. Kylie ran for the fire exit.

*****

The last of the night's clientele had finally left. The staff had cashed up, and the last of the dirty glasses had been put in the industrial dishwasher. Roisin sat over a drink with Brad and Tony.

'Pretty trouble-free night for you two then.'

'Really?!' exclaimed Brad.

'Well, I know Kylie was a bit of a nuisance. But that said.'

'I hope you gave that toe rag what for. He's a worm,' said Tony.

'And you forget the drunk who was fighting in here and the two guys fighting in the street outside?' added Brad.

'Don't be too hard on Kylie, guys. He hasn't had a good life,' pleaded Roisin.

Both men nodded their acceptance of the case for the defence.

'I just don't like seeing you get grief off him, off anyone as it goes,' confessed Tony.

Roisin put her arm around him and squeezed him. Tony melted inside as she teased him.

'Aw, I always wanted a big brother too. You're a sweetheart.'

He thought back to earlier in the night. He saw Roisin handing a piece of paper to a guy whilst she was serving him. He was jealous, of course, but it stopped there, inside his head, inside his heart. It didn't stop him from enquiring, though. He just couldn't help himself.

'You get lucky tonight then, Roisin?'

'How do you mean?'

'I thought I spotted you chatting with a guy. Give him your number, did you?'

Tony tried to make his questioning seem like he was teasing her like he was having a bit of fun. But his question hurt. It wouldn't hurt as much as the answer, though.

'You don't miss a thing, do you?' she laughed.

'Take no notice of him, Roisin. He's just jealous,' Brad teased.

'No, I am not!'

'His name is Jasper. I've seen him in here quite a few times. And yes, he asked me out, and I thought to myself, why not.'
'You make sure he looks after you then,' advised Tony.
'Or he'll have you to answer to, Bruv?' she laughed.
'Yes, yes, he will,' Tony said firmly.

Hollow

Tiffany put her make-up on by candlelight; she always did. She felt it hid whatever imperfections and flaws her face may carry. She was far from what could be called plain, though. Flicking back the ends of her long dark hair across her shoulder, she thought of the night ahead. She put the finishing touches to her lipstick and then slipped her M&S floral midi-waisted dress over her head. She placed her delicate feet into her Miss KG gold snake-printed wedge sandals. Anticipation filled her as she headed down the stairs.

Tiffany hoped tonight would be the night when she finally found the one; the man to end her search. Her quest had found her in all sorts of establishments. This included nightclubs, singles bars, and bog-standard pubs. She had even spent a night playing bingo but to no avail, although she did win ten pounds on a line. The problem was that her hope was often overshadowed by desperation, and that wasn't a good look. Time was no friend either. It was ebbing away at an alarming rate. Her window of opportunity was shrinking away.

Once she had finished preparing for her night out, she hailed an Uber. She checked herself out in the full-length mirror in the hallway. Within five minutes, she was being whisked from her home into the big city. Her excitement rose as the car got closer to the city lights. She felt her phone buzzing inside her Michael Kors handbag; fake, of course, but it looked the part. She wasn't going to answer the call, though; not tonight. There was no good to be had in answering the call.

St Mary Street was bustling. People were all lit by neon signs and streetlamps. The shouts, screams and laughter

rattled around the air. The sound of a busker echoed down the street. She passed the Frantic Fox and shook her head from side to side. She shuddered as she murmured to herself, 'Full of old men. No thanks.'
She advanced further down the road. There was a new venue to be tried tonight. The two doormen looked smart to her, smart enough to entice her into Maddigans. Yes, she was going to try her luck here; this could be the place. Why Mr Right was probably at the bar at that very moment.

*****

Roisin handed the large vodka and coke to Kenney. He managed a smile and took a big gulp of the drink. She smiled back.

'Thirsty then?' she teased.

'It's just been one of those days.'

She'd heard it all before from a thousand punters, but she was still happy to listen.

'You want to tell your Aunty Roisin all about it? That's what I'm here for. The beer, to hear, and then cheer you up!'

'I think you've heard it all before,' Kenney replied.

He was right, she had. He had told her his woes many times, over many drinks. Roisin had one of those faces. She was a good listener. She was sensible and level-headed. She reminded him of someone, someone he loved dearly. He brushed the shoulders of his blue, slim-fit Italian-style suit. He wore a pin-striped shirt underneath it. Roisin loved the way he started to make an effort again.

'Loving the suit, Kenney. Matches your eyes,' she laughed.

'Why, thank you. If only I were ten years younger, eh?'

'Stop it, you! No, I just think it's nice to see you so smart.'

'You're a good woman, Roisin, you know that?'

'Aw shucks … stop it, you tease.'

Kenney grinned. She appreciated his smile as she rarely saw him carry one.

'That's better, see? You're smiling now.'

He nodded at his empty glass.

'You have a wisdom that belies your youth, Roisin. You're like a young Cleopatra.'

She placed the refilled glass in front of him,

'Who?'

'Former ruler of Egypt, a bit before your time, I guess.'

Roisin shrugged her shoulders.

Kenney persevered,

'She had a thing with Julius Caesar?'

'Ah yes, didn't he play for AC Milan?'

'I give up!'

Roisin burst out laughing. She got another smile out of him. He needed cheering up sometimes; well, at all times, actually. She went back to polishing glasses.

'How's Sophie?'

'She's good, still on my back all the time, of course.'

'She cares, Kenney. That's all.'

'I know. I know.'

He turned his back to the bar and surveyed the clientele. *Same old same old,* he thought. Everyone looking for someone or something. He wondered what he was looking for exactly. He didn't really know what he wanted, though. Maybe he didn't even care. The fact was he *was* there, in a bar, on a Saturday night; just looking for something like everyone else.

*****

Tiffany laughed, sipped at her drink, and then fixated on his blue eyes. The joke was lame; Kenney knew that. It explained why his brow was slightly furrowed beneath his head of healthy fair hair.

'You're a funny guy, Kenney. Do you normally drink here?'

He nodded.

'What about you? I guess not, as I'm sure I haven't seen you here before.'

'It's my first time. Hopefully not my last, though.'

Kenney loved Tiffany's flirtatiousness. He was warming to her and could sense she was keen on him too. A sprinkle of guilt hit him as he thought of Sophie back at home.

He checked Tiffany's fingers; there was no ring which was a good start. He thought it too good to be true, though. More drinks were ordered. At no point did either of them notice how quickly they were putting the drinks away. He was enjoying her effervescence. She was just enjoying his conversation, enjoying his presence. The attention he was giving her was very welcome; it had been a long time.

'May I ask if there is anyone in your life, Tiffany?'

She threw him a coy look, and he panicked.

'Sorry, I don't mean to be overfamiliar.'

She laughed again.

'You're ok. There's no one special; not anymore anyway.'

The cryptic response shrouded the moment with a shard of mystery. It nurtured his attraction, though, and he liked that.

'What about you?'

'Likewise, there's no one special in my life.'

Tiffany sensed an underlying sadness in his words. He knew that Sophie would gladly kill him for saying that. But she'd never know.

'What about children?' she asked.

'A daughter, she's pretty much grown up now. But then girls mature faster than us boys, don't they?' he laughed.

'I've no children myself. You're very lucky.'

'Never wanted any?'

'Oh, of course, but I haven't been blessed yet. I feel the time is running away with me too.'

Kenney looked her up and down quickly.

'You've plenty of time,' he stated.

Her brown eyes saddened as she looked away. Kenney worried he had put his size tens in it again. He was always doing it, whatever the scenario.

'Sorry, I didn't mean to upset you.'

'It's ok. It's just meant to be, I guess. The fact is I am desperate for a child. Sorry, listen to me. Let's change the subject. We're supposed to be enjoying ourselves.'

'It's not a problem. Shall we get out of here and find somewhere quieter?' he suggested.

Tiffany put her arm in his, and they turned to leave. As they got to the exit, they were both accosted by a lone figure. The man looked briefly at Kenney and then stared Tiffany down. Her face reddened, and she trembled ever so slightly.

'Oh, it's you,' she uttered.

'Not again, Tiffany, not again!' he replied.

*****

The front door slammed behind them. Tiffany prepared herself for another onslaught. Yes, she'd done it before, so what? She wondered why he was making such a fuss about it all. He knew the score, however painful it was for him. She knew Ed was a good man. She knew he loved her. She still loved him, a bit anyway. She had it all, a nice home, a good job. But it wasn't everything. They used to holiday three times a year but in recent times that had ebbed. They partook in long weekends away now. Their expeditions were turgid affairs, as turgid and dull as their marriage. There wasn't much between them now. A classic case of two people travelling different paths. The other thing was that she was missing something, and it hurt every day. Ed threw the car keys onto the kitchen worktop.

'How much longer is this going to go on, Tiff!?'

She shrugged her shoulders back at him, displaying premier league nonchalance.

'How did you find me?' she asked, irritated.

'Potluck, I guess. Good job I did too. Who was that guy?'

'Kenney, he was a nice man. Looked after me like a true gentleman.'

'Just another guy, like the last one and the one before that! Why do you keep doing this to me?'

'You know why. It certainly isn't for the hell of it, that's for sure! You need to calm down and count yourself lucky I didn't get as far with this one as I did some of the others.'

'Wow, that's some consolation!'

Kicking off her shoes, she opened the fridge door. The cold Pinot Grigio hit the bottom of the glass with a gentle ripple. She dragged the stool from under the breakfast bar and plonked herself on it. The open bottle was held out to him.

'Wanna join me?' she teased.

Her expression was taunting him, but he could also sense her emptiness inside. Her teasing words were hollow.
She continued,

'We could go upstairs if you like, it's been a while, but we could try again. It's not too late to try again, is it, Ed?'

Her desperate tears grew, and her lip trembled. He knew it was pointless. He knew however much he tried, he couldn't give her the one thing she wanted dearly.

*****

Sophie stared quietly at the clock on Alexa. It was 1am, and Kenney still wasn't home. She fumed to herself as she got up from the armchair. He had been getting back into bad habits, out drinking until all hours, and he had been ignoring her texts and calls too. She wondered who the hell he was out with tonight. He'd occasionally come home smelling of perfume. It was never the same brand, though. So, she assumed he didn't see anyone regular. She was sure he had seen other women. The hurt she felt reached incendiary levels at times. She knew he never meant to hurt her, but he did.

A car pulled up outside, and Kenney fell out of it. After battling with the front door key, he entered the living room. Sophie just stared at him. She shook her head at his demeanour.

'Don't start,' he advised her.

He dragged himself into the kitchen and found another drink, another drop to chip away at the pain. Sophie followed him. She said nothing; she didn't need to. Kenney knew this scene very well. He'd lived it a thousand times or more.

'I'd say I'm sorry, but I know you won't believe me.'

She broke her silence.

'This has to stop. I am so scared when you are like this.'

'I'd never hurt you. You know that. I bloody love you, for God's sake!'

'Then why do you do this?'

'I can't get a cure for a broken heart from the doctor, in this day and age too. You'd think they would have found a cure. A tablet or something, to be taken once a day after food. But no, they haven't. So, this is the next best remedy.'

He laughed at his words; his eyes grew moist. Swigging his drink down, he reached for the bottle again. Sophie grabbed the bottle from him.

'Enough! I am so worried about you.'

Kenney slumped to the floor, his back to the freezer door. He started to sob.

'I am so empty without her. Why did she have to go so soon? Why did she have to leave me, leave us?'

Sophie slumped next to him and held him close.

'I miss her too, Dad. There isn't a day I don't think about her. I miss Mum so much.'

Sharing their tears, they held each other close.

Billy and the Ten Bag

It was never easy being Billy Minogue, and tonight was no exception. Minogue wasn't his original surname, of course. He loved the antipodean songstress so much he had it changed by deed poll. The registrar stifled a laugh at the time. He was frequently called Kylie after that, but he knew that was always going to happen. People were so obvious at times.

He hadn't had an easy upbringing. His mum and dad had split up some years back. He had pretty much sofa-surfed since then. He relied on people's goodwill and the trading of ten bags to get him by. He barely spoke with his parents. It was a bit difficult with his mum as she ran off to Norwich with a guy from the Cons Club. As for his dad? He just spent his time drinking in town. Kylie caught up with him now and then for a pint in the Frantic Fox. The fact was that they were living in totally different spheres.

Today had seen him running around trying to keep out of trouble, but it wasn't going well. He'd sold some gear to Desi and Jammo, and now they had been lifted by the law. He also managed to piss off the two bouncers at Maddigans. He offered them free drugs in return for his entry into the bar. Once he managed to get in, Roisin laid into him. But none of that was the real problem. The real issue was two guys and a black Lexus; he needed to avoid them, but he knew they would never be far away. He had enough missed calls from them today to prove that.

He found himself at the door of Dirty Barry's. The night was getting older as he gently rapped at the door. The flat was above a shop in Ely. Kylie didn't know what street he was in. He just knew where it was. The door was yanked open, and a dishevelled figure appeared. His hair was straggled and grey, and he wore a nicotine-stained moustache. He had a grey Adidas hoodie on and ripped skinny jeans. A pair of black sliders graced his feet.

'Fuck off, Kylie!'

'Come on, Barry. I need to lay low.'

'You tried the bed shop?'

Kylie sighed. He put his hand in his pocket. Barry's eyes followed the hand. Kylie pulled out the goods. The ten-bag was snatched out of his hands. Barry opened the door and let him in.

*****

The Lexus was parked up under the bridge in Taff Mead Embankment near the old Avana bakery. The river flowed quietly nearby. Yusuf watched the water taxi head by on its way back to the bay. Sal tucked into the kebab he'd just bought. Another kebab cooled in a bag in the footwell. An overpowering smell of onions filled the car.

'Are you sure that's right?' asked Yusuf.

'Yeah, Dirty Barry just text me!' replied Sal.

'I don't trust that scuzzy fuck man.'

Sal understood what he meant, but he was willing to fight Barry's corner on this occasion.

'Maybe, but what does he have to lose? He knows we'll look after him for giving us the heads-up. I believe him even if he is a low-life.'

'You'd believe the world was flat!'

'You mean it's not?' Sal teased.

'That fucking Kylie owes us,' he added.

Yusuf reached over and snaffled a piece of doner meat from his compadre's kebab. He washed the spicy meat down with a mouthful of Dr Pepper. He checked his rear-view mirror and then started the car up.

'Time to collect then, I reckon.'

'Can we go via my place? I need to drop this other kebab off to Tonya. She'll go bat-shit crazy if I forget.'

'Jeez man, we're supposed to be running a business here! You want me to go to Dirty Barry's via the marina!?'

'If you love me, bro, you will. You know how vexed she can get.'

The rear lights of the Lexus pulled away from the embankment.

*****

Dirty Barry knew it wasn't a good look. There were a few needles in a plastic dish in the sink, along with silver foil. The kitchen worktop wasn't visible as it was covered in empty milk cartons and beer bottles. Empty cereal packets and various bundles of dirty washing also littered the worktop. There was no washing powder or washing-up liquid in sight. The green checked lino was cracked and sticking up in places. Barry couldn't be less worried, though. He was a druggie, and this was druggie chic, not shabby chic.

Kylie wandered around the kitchen, looking quizzical.

'Can I charge my phone, Baz?'

'Yeah, but don't take the piss. Leccy is expensive these days.'

'Yeah, tell that to Martin Lewis, mate. I've seen the bridging wire hanging from your meter in the hall.'

Barry grinned, his yellowing teeth exposing themselves for the first time in a while. He showed Kylie a dark room with an old park bench and a wooden chest of drawers. A set of temporary traffic lights occupied the corner. The place was clearly furnished by Cardiff City Council.

'No place like home, man,' stated Kylie.

Barry sat at one end of the bench and pulled a rollie tin out of his hoodie pocket. He began to roll up, dropping a flaky line of skunk in with some Golden Virginia tobacco. A couple of minutes later, Kylie was toking on the spliff. He handed the joint back to Barry and went back to the kitchen to check his phone.

The small talk between Barry and Kylie was vacuous. They talked about the weather and global warming; the air was asinine and stupefying. Time passed. Kylie didn't notice Barry continually checking his phone. He was too preoccupied with his next move. He couldn't stay at Barry's indefinitely. He reckoned that he would probably catch rickets or scurvy if he did. Barry was getting a little anxious and pulled out his works from the chest of drawers. He produced the ten-bag gifted to him by Kylie; Dirty Barry was about to get dirtier. Kylie didn't ride the horse, but he liked the occasional speedball. Barry finished cooking up and went to hand the needle to Kylie, but he declined. Barry slapped the veins in his arm and aimed the needle at one of them. As it hit the skin, Kylie's phone rang.

'Alright, Maeve. What's the old man done now?'

His face dropped; the news wasn't good. Ending the call, he stood up. Barry was starting to enter his cocoon and becoming incapable of coherency.

'I gotta go, Baz!'

His words were met with drug-induced apathy.

*****

The blues lights flickered against the dirty windows of the Frantic Fox. Kylie hit the entrance as the medics brought the stretcher out. The body on it was completely covered. Maeve was bringing up the rear. She ran to Kylie.

'What are they doing? Where's he going, Maeve?!'

'I'm so sorry, presh, so so sorry.' She squeezed him tightly.

He was in a daze. He knew what he was looking at on the stretcher, but he couldn't accept it.

'I don't get it. What the hell is happening?!'

Maeve held him steady as he tried to break free. He wanted to pull that sheet off his father. He wanted proper confirmation, not just the words of others.

'If it's any consolation, it was very quick. We're guessing it was his heart.'

He buried his head into her shoulder. The ambulance doors were slammed shut on his father. Maeve led Kylie away from the vehicle and into the pub. The hostelry was almost empty except for some of his father's friends. Maeve locked the doors to stop any more punters from entering what was to become a private wake.

Harri Spoons and Shoni Patel shook Kylie's hands. Condolences were plentiful. Dai Scissors sat quietly. He looked up at Kylie and threw his sympathies at him through an ashen frown. Sais Johnny said nothing. Maeve placed four large scotches and an orange juice on the bar. Harri raised his glass.

'To Ianto, long may he run.'

The salutation was muttered by the others, all bar Kylie that is. He was just getting angry with himself. A clichéd raft of thoughts and emotions was rising. He should have spent more time with him. They could have done a lot more together, been there for each other. But they weren't, and Kylie felt like the one to blame. He realised he hadn't managed to tell him the things a son should tell a dad. There was never any time;

the two of them almost occupied different dimensions. The truth was that there was always time, but they were both off doing other things.

This was a defining moment now. He suddenly realised how much he loved his dad. How much they laughed on the rare occasions they met. He remembered how his dad would always pat him on the back and give him a light hug upon seeing him. But it wasn't enough now, and there was nothing he could do about it. He slugged the drink back and put the empty glass back on the bar. He didn't let it go until Maeve had refilled it. She leaned across the bar and beckoned for him to come close.

'He loved you so much. He might not have shown it much, mind. I'll grant you that. But when he was here on his own, he would talk about you all the time.'

Kylie shrugged his weary shoulders. He wasn't sure if he wanted to hear this or not. Either way, Maeve was going to tell him.

'He would tell me how he felt guilty about not doing more for you, doing more with you. He felt bad about the way he and your mum split up. He regretted the arguments that led to them parting. He knew that you witnessed a lot of those fights, and he bemoaned it very much.'

'It's fucked up, Maeve. Here we are, family, and we just let it all fall apart.'

'None of it was your doing, Billy.'

Maeve was one of the few people that called him that. He liked it for a second. It reminded him of who he was once upon a time, before he got messed up, before everything got messed up.

Harri patted Kylie's back as he walked to his chair. Dai Scissors stared into space. He had nothing to say because he didn't know what to say. Sais Johnny got up from his place on the small wooden stool. He approached Kylie. His three-quarter-length leather coat swung from side to side with each step he took. He took Kylie aside.

'I'm sorry about your Ianto, Kylie, but there is something I think you need to know.'

Kylie had an inkling he knew what Sais Johnny was about to say. Johnny tightened his grip on Kylie's shoulder.

'You got to get out of here, man. You got to get away. They're out for you.'

'I know, Johnny.'

'That Yusuf can be a mean little fucker, and I hear you been treading on their toes. Bad move, kiddo.'

Kylie heeded Johnny's words. This wasn't going to end well. He placed the empty glass on the bar and turned to leave. Maeve's concern grew.

'You want to stay at mine tonight, lovely boy?'

'Nah, you're alright, Maeve. I'll crash at a mate's.'

'You take care then, and call me if you need anything at all, you listening? Anything.'

The others bade him farewell. Once outside, he leant back against a bus stop. He wondered how it all got to this, but he knew deep down. He'd made a few careless moves and was going to have to pay for them unless he got out of town for a while. But he had nowhere to go. He pulled the remaining ten-bags out of his pocket. There were five in all. It was time to get rid of them; it was time to move on. Kylie hated mystery trips, though.

Blues and Twos

The body had been hurled out of the vehicle on impact. It had ended up on the hard shoulder some thirty feet away from the wreckage. The smashed-up Lexus was buried into the central reservation. Sergeant Eddie Macari and PC Sheri Cadogan were first on the scene. Eddie immediately checked the person that had been thrown from the car. There was no sign of life; how could there be? Eddie briefly surveyed the wounds. *No one could survive those injuries*, he reckoned. He recognised the man straight away. Sheri was checking on the driver, who was slumped over the steering wheel. He was covered in blood, but she could see he was breathing. The other emergency services, along with some fellow police officers, started arriving.

Eddie and Sheri let the ambulance crew and firemen take over whilst they started to secure the scene. Luckily the A4232 was relatively quiet.

'You ok, Eddie?' she asked.

No matter how many times Eddie had witnessed a scene like this, it still shook him. Sheri knew why, but they had never spoken about it.

'Yeah, yeah, I recognise the guy on the hard shoulder. He's known to us. Sal Bruno, I'm guessing the other guy is his partner Yusuf. Not sure of his surname. Our paths crossed briefly some years back.'

The rescue services were wasting no time. Sheri winced at the sound of the crashed car door being cut off.

'I hope he gets through this. He doesn't look good.'

'I'm wondering why the airbags didn't work?' Eddie asked.

'The car is probably a ringer. Once upon a time, it got nicked and the airbags removed and sold on.'

Sheri's sharpness and street smarts outweighed Eddie's experience on occasion. He had no problem with that. It just attracted him to her more.

'Good work. I see you've been listening to me. We'll make a copper of you yet.'

Sheri smiled back at him. It threw a fraction of light into what was otherwise a grim situation.

'What about the deceased man? What's the story there?'

'He's a dealer, or should I say *was* a dealer? Not your street-level type mind. No, he was a bit sharper than that. Along with Yusuf, they were pretty much running certain parts of the city. There'll be no shortage of people wanting to step into their shoes now.'

'Next of kin?'

Eddie felt sick. This was the one part of the job he truly hated. He fell silent.

'Eddie, are you ok?'

'Yeah, sorry. I was just trying to think. I believe Sal has a girlfriend. She lives in the marina. Not so sure about Yusuf.'

Sheri could see right through him. 'I'll break the news to her,' she offered.

'No, I'll do it.'

'I really don't mind, Eddie. You always do it. It must be a bit painful for you?'

'Why?!' he snapped.

'Sorry, no reason. You do it then.'

Sheri walked away, knowing that she may have crossed a line; some things were strictly taboo.

*****

Tonya watched from her balcony as the tail lights of the police car pulled away. Much as she had hated the police, they had a job to do. The more she thought about it, the more she appreciated how hard it must be to do their job. She got angry with them at first. A refusal to believe the facts blocked the bad news out. Denial and anger enveloped her all at once. But she knew it was no joke. She had fallen to the floor, wailing as she partially accepted the news. The female copper was lovely, though. She helped her up and sat her down. She had made her a strong cup of tea too. The male copper just seemed useless to Tonya. But then, what did she expect him to do?

Her pain was ever-growing now. A knot was forming in her stomach. A tear fell and hit the top of her hand, which was gently trembling. She drew on her cigarette, and more tears fell. She stared out at the marina from her balcony. Questions filled her head; they mingled with her sorrow and fresh heartache. Why did it happen? How did it happen? Was Yusuf driving too fast? Was he using his fucking phone whilst driving?! She knew he did that a lot. She got angry again for a few seconds. Stubbing the cigarette out in the grubby glass ashtray, she wandered back into the flat. Cracking her baby boy's door open, she checked him. He lay there oblivious and now fatherless.

Tonya had always been a worrier, and now that worry was magnified. She feared for her little boy growing up. What would happen to him now? She had to up her game, but no challenge would beat her. Sal was no angel. She wasn't that daft, but he always provided for them. It was easy to turn a blind eye to his dealings, and he never brought any trouble home. He made a point of ensuring that Tonya and the baby had a simple and easy life. Pictures adorned the wall. Sal smiled down from them, accompanied by the baby and herself. Her favourite picture of Sal was the Penarth Pier one, though. It was taken some years back when they first met. He stood proudly in his blue Aquascutum t-shirt. He wore Tommy Hilfiger jeans and white Nike trainers. The sun blazed behind him as he licked away at an ice cream. She took the picture with her iPhone. She liked it so much that she had it printed and framed. He seemed a bit more innocent in those days. How she wanted to go back there now. She wished he had taken a different route in his life, but he hadn't. There was so much to think about. How did one organise a funeral for a start? She had one urgent task first, though. She scrolled through her phone to Sal's mother's number. This wouldn't be good.

*****

The street was cordoned off by the police. A forensics van was parked outside the house, and several police cars were parked up nearby. Eddie and Sheri were called to assist, but it seemed that everything was in hand. They remained parked up in their car nearby.

'Another twenty minutes and we'll scoot off. It's getting near knocking-off time,' Eddie promised.

'Some people, though. No matter how much I see in this job, I never understand how people can do that to another person.'

'Nothing surprises me in this job,' he stated sagely.

'You are truly a savant, Eddie,' she teased.

'It's a cross I have to bear.'

She laughed for a second and then returned her attention to the gravity of the situation.

'What drives someone to murder, Eddie? What drives someone to end another person's life on purpose?'

'I dunno, maybe she burnt his tea?'

'Not funny, and you know it!' she chided.

'Well, I am sure the MIT team will find out. I heard one of the boys saying that the house had more security than Buckingham Palace. CCTV everywhere and more locks and chains on the door than the vault at the Bank of England.'

'I heard she had thirty-five stab wounds.'

'That would do it.'

'I hate it when you are so flippant.'

Eddie nodded at the house.

'Sorry, self-preservation mechanism, I guess. We don't know what led up to what happened over there.'

'Whatever it was, it doesn't warrant such brutality,' she said softly.

'You need to learn to care less. This job will drive you nuts otherwise.'

She soaked up his words. But there was more behind Eddie's attitude to all this. He checked his phone.

'Not long to go now. Any plans for tomorrow?'

'Not really. I find Sundays so boring, don't you?'

'I prefer to work them, to be honest, always a bit quieter than Saturdays.'

'What are you up to tomorrow then?'

'Walking up Pen-Y-Fan.'

'Sounds a bit energetic to me.'

'I love it. Me and Eleri used to go up there a lot.'

Sheri froze for a second. It was the first time she could remember him talking about his wife. She knew she had passed away. His words left her speechless for a moment. Her mind rallied around for a response. Her mouth ran dry as she spoke.

'What was she like?'

But he just ignored her. Eddie took one last glance at the scene of the crime and started the car up. Another shift was over, and another day of catching the bad guy was over.

*****

She used to call it the Golden Arches; Eddie loved that. Eleri could be hilariously funny when she wanted. It was one thing he loved so much about her. He grinned to himself as he stirred his coffee.

Sheri placed a bacon roll and a coke on the table and sat down. It was their ritual after every Saturday night shift. They'd go and get refreshments before going home. She unwrapped the bacon roll and could sense Eddie looking at it.

'Want a bite?'

The aroma was driving him mad.

'No thanks and neither should you! Bad for you, that is.'

'You saying I'm fat?!'

He knew she was far from that. He was still battling to contain his feelings for her. It felt wrong. He felt he didn't deserve to be happy again. He also knew how ridiculous that was.

'Of course, I'm not. I'm just thinking of your health.'

She bit into the roll with vigour and grinned at him. He stirred away at his coffee again, and she swallowed hard.

'I'm sorry, Eddie.'

'For what?'

'For earlier, I may have said a couple of things I shouldn't have. Sorry.'

'There's no need to apologise for anything. I know you mean well.'

Silence grew between them. This wasn't awkward at all. Eddie finished the last of his coffee and looked out into the darkness.

'You would have liked her.'

'Eleri?'

Eddie nodded.

'She would have liked you too. She was that sort of person. She loved everyone, and everyone loved her.'

Sheri felt a sense of honour. She stayed silent as he continued.

'She was smart and funny. She loved the outdoors. One time we got stuck on Sully Island. We didn't take any notice of the warning signs. We walked over to it, and then the tide came in. I took some stick at the station for that one, I can tell you!'

She laughed.

'Do you mind me asking what happened to her?'

He paused, but he knew he was safe to talk about it with Sheri. If he broke down, she'd understand.

'Drunk driver. Wiped her straight out.'

'Oh, Eddie, I'm so sorry.'

'It's ok, no need to be.'

'Have you got a photo of her?' she enquired.

'I stopped carrying her photo a couple of years back now. I felt it was stopping me from moving on. It's hard to let the past go, but it was the past. I have to deal with it like that. It probably goes someway to my flippant attitude you pointed out earlier.'

Sheri laughed again.

'I'll never forget her, of course,' he added.

'Of course, you won't, Eddie.'

'I want to move on, but I feel guilty. Is that stupid?' he quizzed.

'Not at all, but you deserve to be happy. We all do, come to that. Have you been involved with anyone since? Sorry, I'm overstepping.'

'Please, you're not. It's ok. Not really.'

Eddie wondered if he should throw down his hand. *To hell with the consequences*, he reasoned. He hadn't talked with anyone like this in many years. He felt the moment was suitably intimate, even if the conversation had been about Eleri. He knew deep down that she wouldn't mind, that she would give him her blessing. Life was too short, as the evening shift had proved. The time was now.

'There is someone I have feelings for. I'm not sure she is aware of it, though.'

Sheri put her hand on his.

'I think you'll find she is.'

The Needle and the Damage Done

Marco thought she was a stupid bitch, but she entertained him at times. He agreed to meet her today because he had nothing or no one better to do. He scooped his floppy dark quiff back over his head and threw his face up at the sky. Lifting a cigarette to his lips, he felt regal, the king of all bastards. He stretched his long legs out on the steps of the Senedd as he viewed Cardiff Bay and the marina beyond.

He reasoned that she was probably getting herself ready to meet him at that very moment. She was probably applying potions and powders to try and win him over once and for all. He smiled to himself, like that would ever happen. He had no intention of getting seriously involved with her or any other woman, come to that. He reckoned ties were for funerals. They certainly weren't for him.

He checked the time. Their rendezvous was an hour away. Four o'clock was the agreed time. They'd argued about the venue, though. Marco wanted to meet up in town, but she said no. She reasoned that if they met up in town at that time, they would end up drinking far too much too soon. So, they compromised. The plan was to meet up in Mermaid Quay, have a light meal and then hit town. Marco was dead against any compromise in truth, but if it meant him getting his way with her, it would be worth it.

Two German tourists walked up to him and asked for directions to Cardiff Castle. He told them he wasn't sure, lying through his peroxide-whitened teeth. They thanked him anyway and walked away. His phone gave a short buzz in his back pocket. He knew it was her; it had to be. He lit another cigarette; always best to keep them waiting.

*****

Marco stood with his back to the bar. He sipped at his White Russian, his third since he got to Maddigans. He'd show the bitch. Her text informed him that she was going to be about an hour late. He didn't bother responding. Marco took it upon himself to start without her. He was fixated on a blonde woman standing at the other end of the bar. She seemed to be alone. His arrogance levels reached new heights as he approached her.

'Do I know you?' he asked.

She knew a pick-up line when she heard one but decided to play along. She smiled back at him.

'I don't know, do you? I don't come here often before you ask.'

Marco smiled; he was in. This was too easy.

Time passed by. The beats flew around their heads as their drinking and laughing increased. Her name was Sian. She was an artist and admitted to being slightly older than him. That was all he needed to know, to be honest. He was on a mission that didn't include getting her life story. He thought she seemed keen; she kept remarking on his skin and complexion. This was going to be a doddle. She was just another girl, another trophy for the cabinet. His original date was total history now; until he got a firm poke in his back. He turned to receive a full glass of wine in his face. His assailant turned and left with haste. Sian didn't seem surprised at the incident. She stood and watched Marco as he wiped the wine from his forehead.

'Someone you know?' she teased.

'She's a fucking mad bitch, been stalking me for ages. I told her it was over so many times, but what can you do?'

They finished their drinks before Sian suggested they move on.

*****

Charlie watched as the last of the soap suds disappeared down the plug-hole of the kitchen sink. There was a knock at the front door. He looked at the clock on the wall. It looked back smugly and proudly told him it was very late. He sighed. He knew exactly who was behind the knocking. It had to be her, Jodi. Only she could be found knocking at his door at this hour. It is only her that he would ever open it for at such an hour too. Jodi was his neighbour, but she was more than that to him, although she didn't know it. Opening the door, he found her leaning against the doorframe. Her make-up had run where she had been crying, and her long dark hair was soaking wet.

'Sorry,' she whimpered.

'Jodi, what a surprise!'

'Don't lie. You knew it would be me. Who else would it be?'

She had a red rain-soaked coat draped around her fine shoulders. Rainwater had crawled a good few inches up the denim at the bottom of her bootleg-jeaned legs.

'Come on in. I'll get you a towel to dry yourself off.'

She fell through the doorway. Her blue eyes were framed by red eyelids. But it wasn't just the crying that had turned them that way; she was also very drunk.

'He's done it again! How could he?!'

'He' was Marco, Jodi's miscreant of a part-time boyfriend. Charlie always regarded him as a part-time lover. Jodi and Marco had spent as much time apart as together since they became an item. He never understood why she bothered with such a loser. He had never treated her right. Charlie knew for a fact he could look after her better than that bastard did. That was all he wanted to do; just look after her forever. He helped her into the living room. She kicked her heels off, threw her coat on the floor, and then slumped onto the sofa. Charlie lifted her legs onto it and made sure she had ample cushions to lay her head on.

'You're a very nice man, Charlie. You know that?'

He smiled back at her.

'Yeah, I know that,' he laughed.

'Not like him. He's a complete bastard!' she moaned.

'What's he done now, Jodi?'

'What hasn't he done!? I should find myself someone better. In fact, I deserve someone better!'

Charlie wanted to say something but couldn't bring himself to do it. He went to the bathroom to get a towel for her. When he got back, she sat up, furiously composing a text message on her phone.

'Is that advisable? You'll only regret it. You should let the dust settle for tonight. Things will look different in the morning.'

Jodi was oblivious, lost in a haze of fuming hatred for Marco's earlier assignation.

'Any danger of getting a drink around here?' she demanded.

'Certainly, I'll pop the kettle on now; white, no sugar, yeah?'

'Hilarious! Now, if you would be so kind, I'll have a glass of wine, please!'

He acquiesced and went to the kitchen to execute Jodi's instructions. She was fully reclined on the sofa when he returned. She was staring at the ceiling, hoping it would spell out a solution to her love woes. Charlie placed the drink next to her on the floor. He then positioned himself in the armchair opposite. The silence lasted for a few minutes.

'You're a nice man, Charlie...'

Her voice softened as she continued,

'… a very very nice man indeed.'

'Am I?'

She took a sip of her wine and swallowed slowly.

'You think I only ever come here when I want to bitch about him, don't you?'

'As if!' Charlie lied.

'I mean, I know it probably seems that way, but I like coming to visit you. You're a very nice man.'

'So you keep saying.'

'And he's a bastard!' she rasps.

'Yes, quite. How is Marco these days? I haven't seen him since the police took him away from your front door the other week.'

'That was a misunderstanding!'

'Yes, Lord only knows why his hand slipped and punched a hole in your front door. Mind you, doors aren't what they're used to be these days … wafer thin they are.'

She soaked up his sarcasm.

'Alright, so he's not perfect.'

'So what's he done this time?'

'Who?'

'The bastard formerly known as Marco.'

'Well, I met him in town earlier. I told him I'd be late but that I'd meet him in Maddigans.'

'That place is a dump if you ask me.'

'Christ, Charlie! You're so stiff it's a wonder you don't snap when you cough! You need to get out and enjoy yourself more.'

'Like you?'

'Yeah, anyway. I got there only to find him all but sticking his tongue down some blonde tart's throat!'

Her eyes began to well up.

'Don't go upsetting yourself now.'

'Upsetting myself?! Upsetting myself?! Wouldn't you be upset if you caught your boyfriend with his hands on some blonde tart's tits?!'

'Really?'

'Well, no, I may have exaggerated a bit. But the intention was there!'

She finished her glass of wine with one gulp and held the glass out demandingly at Charlie.

'That's not the answer, Jodi.'

She shook the glass at him; he gave in to her demand.

'You're a nice man, Charlie.'

'So, what did you do?'

'I threw a glass of wine in his face.'

'Jesus! What was his response?'

'I didn't hang around to find out.'

Charlie stifled a laugh. She got riled,

'You think it's fucking funny!?'

'No, of course not.'

'I don't know what to do. I love him so much.'

'Maybe you need to find a better man. One who knows how to use a knife and fork, or one who knows the right way to sit on a toilet perhaps.'

Jodi grinned.

'He's not that bad, Charlie.'

'Mmm, perhaps so. How long have you two been together?'

'Eighteen months now.'

'What about that time he had to "go away"?'

'He was never guilty! He was framed!'

'Everyone loves a bad boy, don't they?'

'Oh, don't start with that "all women love a bastard" shit!'

'Eighteen months. Time flies when you're having fun, I guess. So, on how many occasions have you split up during this time?'

'Twenty-one … I think. I don't count that time I caught him coming out of a lap-dancing bar. He was under a lot of stress at the time. We had a row, but that was all. Any chance of a sarnie? I'm starving.'

Charlie returned to the kitchen.

'You're a very nice man you are.'

He returned with a sandwich. Her phone beeped. He got mildly annoyed.

'I suppose it's the bastard sending you a bastard text apologising for being the bastard that he is?'

'Yes,' she replied.

'The bastard.'

'Aw bless him. He says he's sorry. Says it won't happen again. He says he looks forward to seeing me tomorrow for a late lunch.'

Charlie couldn't help but wonder how many lives this twat had.

'All's well that ends well then.'

She reached out for her drink and raised it slowly to her lips. She took a few sips and reclined again. He watched as she gently closed her eyes. He knew exactly what was going to happen next. He had seen it so many times before. She turned on her side, clamped her hands into her chest, and then fell asleep. He decided to keep vigil for an hour or so. He listened to her gentle breathing as she slept. He thought of how much he loved her, yet how afraid he was to tell her. This was because he was a nice man, as she said. But being nice was getting him nowhere; nowhere at all.

Charlie thought back to when he first met Jodi. He figured it must have been three years since. It was the day he moved into the avenue. She kindly kept the removal guys and himself supplied with tea and biscuits all day. She seemed livelier then. Marco had crushed some of the spirit out of her since she started seeing him. Charlie remembered their first big public argument. He was sitting watching the television one evening when he heard the slamming of a car door. He went to the window to see Jodi angrily walking away from a taxi. Marco sat inside it. He was shouting at her through the passenger window. He seemed to be enjoying the profanities pouring from his foul mouth. After the taxi had left, Charlie took it upon himself to go and see if she was alright; but she wouldn't answer the door.

And now here she was again. Charlie had lost count of the number of times she had called in on him at some ungodly hour. But he always welcomed her. He loved nothing more than falling into her world, however upset or drunk she was. He continued to watch her sleep. There was a gentle purr emanating from her lips as she lay still. He went to the spare bedroom and pulled the quilt off the bed. He returned and gently lay it over her. He left her and went to his bed.

The following morning Charlie found the sofa empty except for the quilt. A wine glass with its stale contents sat beside it. She had gone, but she had left him a hastily scribbled note. He read it slowly.

Thanks for being there and listening, hope I wasn't a nuisance!

The note was signed with a flourishing letter 'J' and a huge kiss. As he held it in his hand, he wished he could kiss her for real. But he knew that all he could do was wait for the next knock at the door.

*****

The sunlight found its way through the crack in the curtains. It licked at Marco's face as he lay face down across the strange bed. The pastel-coloured quilt covered his backside and right leg. His left leg dangled over the edge of the bed. He didn't recognise his surroundings at all. The white clock flashed the time at him, amongst other details. He could sense a weak smell of coffee from downstairs and could hear a couple of muffled voices. He attempted to move, but his head had the whole of the Welsh National Opera rehearsing inside it. He flopped his head back on the bed. He felt strange, numb almost. He heard laughter from downstairs and decided to try and shape up. He rolled over the bed and sat up. He felt discomfort in his lower back, more specifically on his buttocks. He didn't recall much of what happened when they got back to Sian's house the previous night. Maybe she was into S&M. Maybe she had an armoury of sex toys. But his recall didn't suggest so. He crept across the landing to the bathroom. The talking had ceased below him.

*****

Sian was sitting in the kitchen when Marco ran in screaming. He was apoplectic.

'Look what you've done! You mad bitch!'

Sian turned to the man sitting on the other side of the kitchen table and shrugged her shoulders.

'Why would you do this!?' Marco shouted.

The tattoo was perfectly inked across his buttocks.

The man smiled.

'Wow! Nice piece of work, Sian!'

'I'm glad you like it, Charlie.'

Marco's rage continued.

'You better get this fucking removed!'

She frowned at him.

'Language, Marco! Now, let me introduce a friend of mine. His name is Charlie.'

Marco scrutinised the man.

'Don't I know you?'

Charlie shrugged back at him.

'I doubt it. I'm a very nice man, whereas you are a piece of dirt. That tattoo, however, it's a bloody masterpiece.'

Marco stormed out of the kitchen and back upstairs to collect his things. Charlie couldn't fight his smiles. Sian fired the kettle back up.

'He was easy to find, Charlie, his sort always is. Getting him here was a doddle, a few 'extra strong' drinks, and he was putty in my hands.'

'Maybe women will see him for what he is now.'

'Maybe,' she replied.

Shots

'Don't make yourself a victim of regret, Aaron!'

He looked towards the Bristol Channel, it's eddying current flashing white foam back at him. Kayla was hitting a particularly stubborn nail square on the head with her words. He looked from the end of the pier into the water below. His head was starting to spin.

'It's not that easy,' he fought back.

Kayla reloaded.

'If it was easy, it wouldn't be worth it.'

She tried to reign in her desperation; she just wanted it all sorted.

The morning breeze threw itself around their heads as he sighed heavily. He rubbed at his crop of tight dark hair. Sharply groomed, he was the one for her; she couldn't imagine being with anyone else. His clothes were equally as sharp. His tight-cut, straight-leg jeans, and Barbour ankle boots, were topped off by a black Tacchini polo shirt. Kayla was beginning to edge on petulance now as she stepped up her interrogation.

'Do you love me, Aaron, or have I just been a casual bit on the side all this time?'

Her blonde hair was tied into a top knot which wobbled back and forth as she continued in her animation. Her blue eyes pierced through his.

'You know I do, but I love her too,' he weakly responded.

'Yeah, well, this is real life now, not the playground. This is serious adult shit, Aaron!'

'I don't know how you can be so callous. I feel so fucking guilty, what with all this. Not to mention what's happening in a couple of weeks.'

'She'll get over it.'

'Get over it?! Get over me cancelling the wedding to run off with you? Her closest friend?!'

'You forgot to add maid of honour too. Anyway, it'll give everyone something to talk about. I don't care. I just want you, no one else, just you ... period!'

'I don't know, Kayla. Fuck, I hate all this.'

'Look, Aaron, you're a good man, and by that, I mean honest.'

'Honest!? How do you work that out? I have been seeing you behind her back for eighteen months now.'

'Then do the honourable thing and tell her before it's too late. If you don't, then I will. It's the only thing to do.'

'No, I'll tell her. You keep quiet. It's the only way,' he instructed.

'You don't regret what we have, do you?' she enquired cutely.

He moved in closer to her and kissed her forehead.

'No, of course not. I am just worried about the fallout.'

'I've thought about that. I got a friend down west Wales. They got a caravan we can have for a while. No one will know where we are.'

'And how will we survive?'

Kayla squeezed him closer.

'We'll live off the fruits of love, won't we.'

Aaron felt her squeeze loosen. She gently pushed him away.

'So, get it done! Tell her tonight!'

'But it's her hen night, and more to the point, you're going to be there with her!'

'Yeah, don't you just love the danger? Just call the wedding off tonight, and we'll tell her about us in a few days. That way, I get to enjoy the evening.'

'You familiar with the word *schadenfreude*?'

'Is that like a vegetarian thing or something?'

Kayla smiled, kissed him on the cheek and then turned away. 'Speak later, lover.'

He watched as she paraded down the pier back towards Penarth Promenade.

*****

'Your father would be so proud!' April cried.

Mimi gently strutted around the shop. She paraded the ivory A-Line wedding dress with unbridled anticipation. Stopping for a second, her eyes welled up gently.

'I wish he could be there, Mum.'

'So do I, lovely girl, so do I. But he is watching over you. You know that.'

She took brief comfort from her mother's words; Mimi looked into the mirror again. She gently stroked the lace sleeve. Her expression turned to happiness. He'd be so made up; she knew he would.

The shop assistant placed the dazzling garment gently into a dress bag. Mimi and her mother sat and waited.

'So, I take it you'll be drinking far too much tonight, strippers and midgets and all that?'

'No, Mum. Just a few drinks in Canton and then on to town.'

'You'll be drinking them stupid shots too, I guess?'

Mimi raised her eyes back at her mother.

'It's a hen do, so I guess yes, there will be shots. Why don't you come along?'

'I'm a bit old for all that. Anyway, you heard from your husband-to-be today?'

'He's got a name, you know.'

'I know, I know.'

'He'll probably turn up at some point.'

'Well, now that's not right!'

'I want him to; I know I'll get home safely if he turns up!'

'You sound like you don't trust yourself. Maybe I will come along, actually.'

'Well, go dust off your handbag and glad rags when we are finished here. It'll be a blast.'

The shop assistant coughed gently to alert them both that the dress was ready, as was the bill. April took her purse out of her black patent handbag, Mimi stretched out an arm.

'It's ok, Mum. I have the money for this,' she offered.

'No, I insist.'

'But we've been saving for this. We don't expect you to pay for anything.'

'It was your father's wish, and he can't be here, so I am taking care of it. He put a bit aside for you every week from a young age. Although, if he had his way, the money wouldn't be spent on your wedding, and you know why.'

Mimi smiled back at her.

'Because there was no man good enough to marry his daughter?'

'Exactly!'

They laughed, Mimi felt warm inside, April felt sick.

*****

The ball hit the post and went out for a corner kick. The crowd roared the players on. Daryl shouted along with them from his seat in the Canton End. Aaron seemed preoccupied. He just looked down at his phone.

'Shit, man. That should have been 1-0!' exclaimed Daryl.

Aaron looked up.

'Yeah, so close.'

'What's up with you, man? You barely watched any of the game. What's upsetting you?'

'Upsetting me?!'

'Yeah, you chucked half your burger away before the game for a start. That's not you, man!'

The corner kick came flying into the six-yard box. The centre-forward buried it into the net. The crowd exploded around them both. Daryl was shaking Aaron by the shoulder. The cry went out.

'BLUEBIRDS! BLUEBIRDS! BLUEBIRDS!' shouted Daryl.

Aaron smiled and then returned to his quiet desperation. The teams retook their positions for the kick-off.

'Something you want to tell me, mate?' Daryl asked.

'Nope.'

'You sure?' Daryl quizzed.

'I'm sure, just got a lot to sort with the wedding and that.'

'Can't be easy.'

Aaron just wanted him to shut up, plain and simple. He loved Daryl like a brother and had asked him to be his best man. The game restarted. Aaron sat back in his seat. For a brief second, he wished it was an electric one. Maybe someone could flick a switch and take him out of this situation for good.

Daryl continued,

'No sir, can't be easy at all, lots to arrange, flowers, cars, the reception might be tricky too?'

Aaron wanted to gaffer tape Daryl's mouth up now. He was getting tired of this.

'Will you drop it? I just want to watch the game.'

'Sorry, I'm sure,' Daryl responded.

'And what do you mean by the reception being tricky?' Aaron snapped.

'I was thinking about the reception you're going to get when you tell Mimi about Kayla.'

Aaron flew out of his seat and straight down the stairs. Daryl trailed him right out of the stadium and into the car park.

*****

Aaron stared into his pint. The bubbles rose totally carefree to the top of the amber fluid. Daryl sat next to him. They both studied their glasses. It had taken them ten minutes to get from the seats in the stadium to the seats in the Ninian Park pub. The afternoon trade was quiet. It would be until the game finished. They held their gaze at the drinks.

'It's amazing stuff, isn't it?' Daryl stated.

'What is?'

'The amber fluid of course. It has tremendous power when you think about it. It can make a person loving, or it can get them vexed, or..'

'How did you know?' interrupted Aaron.

'I don't know. I could just tell. Your body language when you were around her, maybe. I haven't been your best mate since childhood for nothing. I know you; I know what you're thinking, what you're feeling.

Plus, I have always considered myself a bit of a mind reader, especially when it concerns you.'

'Maybe you should stop being so fucking nosy then?!' Aaron chided.

Daryl laughed. Concern gripped Aaron's face.

'Does anyone else know?' he asked.

Daryl took a sip of his beer.

'A couple of the boys mentioned it on your stag do a couple of weeks back. I told them they were all barking mad to think such a thing.'

'Fuck!' he exclaimed.

'Precisely, it's all pretty fucked up, I'd say.'

'I don't know how it has come to this.'

'I think you do, mate. Still, it's too late for that. Do you love her?'

'Who, Mimi or Kayla?'

'That response sums it up, I guess. You aren't even sure.'

'I think I love them both.'

'How did it all start? You must have known you were walking into a minefield.'

'Yeah, but I was kind of hoping if I stepped lightly enough, I wouldn't set any off.'

'Idiot!'

'Precisely.'

'So, what are you going to do?' Daryl asked.

'You tell me? I hate all this.'

'That Kayla is a bit hot mind, but she scares me. I'd imagine she can be quite intimidating, especially in the bedroom.'

'It can be interesting at times, to be honest.'

'I bet!'

Aaron picked up his beer and shook his head gently.

'I said I'd meet up with Mimi tonight.'

'On her hen do?' Daryl quizzed.

'It's what she wants. And Kayla is obviously going to be there. She wants me to tell her the wedding is off.'

Daryl's eyes bulged. He gulped heavily.

'TONIGHT!?'

'Yeah, tonight.'

'That's some situation!'

Aaron's phone buzzed; it was Mimi.

'I got to make a call, bruv.'

*****

The L-Plates hung limply around her neck as Mimi slurped another glass of Prosecco. One of them had a hole in and what looked like blood on it. The fact was it was chilli sauce from the kebab she had attacked before entering the nightclub. Kayla stood with her back to the bar smiling at the state of the bride-to-be. She slammed the empty shot glass on the bar next to her Radley handbag. She loved every minute; she found the whole thing sublime. Kayla couldn't pinpoint when she began to hate her former best friend. She figured it was probably when Mimi started seeing Aaron, though. Kayla had loved Aaron for many years but never made a move. That was far too scary to consider. And then Mimi beat her to it; the dream was over until tonight.

It had been an interesting evening so far. Mimi had broken down weeping on a couple of occasions. No one figured why apart from the fact it was a very emotionally-charged evening. They all knew she missed her dad. They knew how much she wanted him to be there. Kayla had held back and treated the whole evening as expected. She had danced with Mimi in the various venues they had frequented.

Mimi wouldn't have suspected a thing. There had been a flashpoint in a pub earlier when two of the party had a spat. It was one of those drunken rows between two people where there was no actual reason behind it. It was over as quick as it started. Both girls were now dancing together, oblivious to whatever the flashpoint was. Kayla suddenly found April at her side. Mimi's mother looked on in earnest at the goings-on. Kayla threw her a false smile.

> 'She's having a great night, isn't she!? We're going to give her a good send-off before she gets the old ball and chain tied to her ankle.'

April threw an erroneous smile back at her. Both knew and respected the mutual dislike between them. They'd lived with it for a while now. In all fairness, April was wary of everything and everyone around her these days. She'd known Kayla since she was a child. She'd been a good kid but had grown into an over-confident and arrogant young woman. April ordered herself a shandy; she knew she couldn't stop everyone's mindless drinking. She could have tried, but it would have been a party-pooping waste of time and effort. April would just be there to pick up the pieces.

Mimi drunkenly plotted her course to the bar where Kayla stood, like the smiling assassin she was.

'Kayla, Kayla, Kayla!'

Mimi threw her arms around Kayla's neck.

> 'Kayla, I fucking love you, I do! But it's never going to be the same, is it, once I marry Aaron?'

Kayla closed in on Mimi's face and kissed her full on the lips. She knew the kiss to be the last between them; Aaron would see to that when he arrived. She had loaded the gun and handed it to him earlier that day. He was going to finish it; he was going to give Mimi both barrels. Then and only then could Kayla move on with him. She viewed Mimi as expendable now, just detritus in her rear-view mirror.

'I know you love me, presh. But yes, I guess there will be changes. Fewer nights out like this for a starter!'

Mimi pulled away and knocked Kayla's bag from the bar. April retrieved the bag and placed it back on its perch. Mimi was oblivious. She focussed her gaze and looked around the club.

'Aaron should be here by now.'

'I haven't seen him, babes. He'll be here, though. I'm sure he won't let you down.'

Kayla smiled inside. She couldn't wait to see the big reveal. She couldn't wait to see the heartbreak. It was the only thing she came for.

Mimi fixed her drunken stare back onto Kayla.

'It'll never be the same between us, but I still fucking loves you.'

Kayla smiled back, but inside all she had was hatred.

'We all got to move on, babes. It's called progress.'

A momentary silence filled the air. There was a shout from behind them both. The rest of the hens had spotted Aaron as he arrived. He arrived at Mimi's side among the whooping and hollering of the women. Kayla's moment had come. Aaron was going to do what she had told him. A drama-filled scene filled her head. Aaron would take Mimi's hand and lead her somewhere quieter; somewhere he could tell her it was over. He would leave the club alone, and Kayla would follow shortly after. Mimi would be left in the clutch of loving arms of her friends. She fixed Aaron with a steely stare, which he returned. She was willing him on. She was willing him to finish it, to slice Mimi's heart in two with his words, to pull the trigger. April remained nearby, guarding her little girl.

But she didn't need protecting, and the punch she threw at Kayla's jaw proved as much.

'How could you!? How dare you even think you'd get away with this?'

Kayla picked herself back up. She was shaken.

Mimi continued,

'I should kick the living hell out of you, but I'm far better than that. I have known about you two for a while now. But I stuck with it because I believed that Aaron would see sense eventually. You were a distraction, that's all!'

'He doesn't love you, you stupid girl!' Kayla fought back.

Aaron grabbed at Mimi's hand and squeezed gently,

'Come on, let's go.'

'Not yet, Romeo!' she barked back. She was sobering up at an incredible rate now.

'I knew about it all, but I banked on the fact that true love would cut through all your bullshit! You see, this man took a walk on the other side of the road for a while with you. He walked down that fucking avenue of deceit. But it wasn't for him in the end. So it looks like you'll be taking that caravan in west Wales on your own now. So do us all a favour and fuck off as soon as you can!'

Aaron led Mimi out of the club. Kayla was left at the bar alongside Mimi's mother. April finished her shandy and then spoke.

'I hope you learned something from this debacle. You should never underestimate the power of true love. The passing of Mimi's father struck her hard, but it made her harder. And if something is worth fighting for … well, then you better make sure you're a good fighter.'

The Gumshoes Blues

Harvey Rachman didn't dress that well for a millionaire. Davy wasn't bothered as long as he paid his bill.

'I love her, of course, but Alana has a record for cheating on me.'

Davy nodded back at him.

'She's what you might call a bit of a livewire.'

A spoiled brat more like, Davy reckoned. Rachman probably provided an expense account in every store in London for her. Davy had investigated similar cases in the past, and none of them had ended well.

'I'll need some pictures, Mr Rachman, and some idea of the places she frequents.'

'I never bloody know where she is!'

'If you can think of anywhere, it'll help.'

'You're an investigator, aren't you?! So, investigate!'

The private investigation business had been quiet for Davy Payne of late. He was therefore quite keen to help Rachman out for his usual fee plus expenses. Davy relaxed his wiry frame back into his creaking leather swivel chair. He stared across the desk at Rachman as he gently swivelled from side to side.

'How many times before?'

Rachman looked puzzled. Davy expanded his question,

'How many times has she cheated on you before?'

The millionaire bowed his snowy-haired head for a moment. The squeaking of the swivel chair seemed to increase in volume. Davy didn't know if he was adding up Alana's indiscretions in his head, or if the question was too painful for him to answer. Rachman coughed.

'Let's say it is more than half a dozen times.'

'And what makes you think she's doing it now?'

'I just know, and I can't take it anymore. If she is, then this will be the last time, the last time she makes a bloody fool of me!'

Davy stopped swivelling in the chair. Rachman reached inside his jacket and pulled out a photo; she was stunning. Her blonde hair surrounded a face so mind-blowingly striking; she had razor-sharp cheekbones. Her eyes were a deep ocean blue, and her lips were so full; she was a vision. He could understand Rachman's insecurity.

'You asked about her whereabouts, about places she liked to frequent? Well, I know she is going to Cardiff on Friday afternoon. She is leaving from Paddington around 2pm. As far as I know, she is travelling alone, visiting friends apparently. God knows who.' Rachman got up from the chair; he reached inside his jacket and then threw a wad of bank notes onto the desk. 'This should cover your expenses.'

Davy looked at the money. Remaining silent, he looked up at Rachman before returning his gaze to the money on his desk.

'I'll send you some more photos of Alana when I get home.' advised Rachman.

*****

The departures board proudly displayed the thirty-minute delay to the Cardiff train. Davy sat reading a newspaper or at least pretending to. He wore shades and a navy baseball cap. The matching hooded top and tracksuit bottoms gave him anonymity. He could see Alana sitting outside a coffee shop across the concourse; she oozed opulence. A short white leather jacket draped itself around her shoulders. She wore a matching white mini skirt and the finest Louboutin heels. She picked up her mobile phone and spoke. As soon as she terminated the call; she started texting someone, a huge smile radiating from her face.

It was an uneventful trip apart from the very annoying lady sitting next to Davy. She spent the whole journey on her phone. Everyone in the carriage knew about her new grandson and her older daughter's divorce. The woman's mother's hip problems became public consumption too. As hard as he tried, Davy's heavy sighing did not deter the woman at all.

Within a couple of hours, he was holed up in his hotel room. He had followed Alana from the station. He watched her enter Driscoll's Hotel on Custom House Street. Waiting for half an hour, he then walked through the same door. Paying cash up front ensured that he got a room at the hotel too.

He freshened up and threw on a pair of jeans in place of his tracksuit bottoms. He swapped the baseball hat and hooded top for a t-shirt and beige three-button linen jacket. He then ran a comb through his hair. It was time to track down the truth. He passed Alana in the reception area. She sashayed from the lift doors to the reception desk. He overheard her talking to the receptionist.

'Could you get me a taxi to Club Paradis, please?'
Davy made his way out of the hotel and took a brief stroll away from the hotel. After a few minutes, he stopped to check the location of Alana's destination on his phone. It would seem Club Paradis was a few blocks back from Mermaid Quay; it was walkable.

The inside of the establishment was dark but seductive and airy. Hints of incense hung in the air. Candles occupied each table. The music was a mix of Café del Mar Chillout and Euro Jazz. Couples sat at tables gazing into each

other's eyes. Davy looked a little out of place, and his entrance to the establishment was not without issue. The doorman was reluctant to let him in alone, but once again, money talked.
A single purple candle flickered in the middle of his table. He looked around for Alana, but she wasn't to be seen. Sipping at a glass of mineral water, he noticed her suddenly glide past. She looked resplendent in her azure blue summer dress. Her hair playfully bounced around her shoulders. It was clear that the bar staff knew her well. She was greeted warmly by all. Davy looked on in wonderment; she was breathtaking.
A bubbly pink cocktail was thrown under her nose before she could take her seat at the bar.
Davy's phone vibrated in his pocket.

'Any luck yet? Any news at all? Have you seen her?'

Davy threw a quick response back at Rachman.

'No, give it time!'

He didn't know why he lied to Rachman; he just did. He ordered another drink, something a bit stronger this time. She excited him. She was now talking on her phone whilst looking directly at Davy. It unnerved him. As his second drink arrived, Alana got up from her stool and began to walk in his direction. She stopped in her tracks at his table and smiled down at him.

'Mind if I join you?'

His blood pumped speedily around his veins.

'Not at all.'

He stood up and pulled out a chair for her. Her fragrance intoxicated him.

'You look familiar?' she enquired.

'No, I just have one of those faces.'

They both laughed.

'Can I get you a drink?' he asked.

Alana smiled back. She placed her hand on his knee.

'Are you trying to get me drunk, sir?'

Rachman was right. She wasn't backward in coming forwards.

'Perish the thought!' he replied.

Davy beckoned the waiter. Alana looked deep into Davy's eyes again.

> 'That's a pity, you look like a nice guy, and a nice girl like me needs to have a bit of fun. A place as ambient and romantic as this is ideal for such a thing, don't you think?'

She was casting a spell with each word; each glance into his eyes burned a little bit more into his soul. He was supposed to be there in a professional capacity, but she was totally irresistible. The drinks arrived in quick succession, and more drinks after that. They laughed, drank, danced, drank, danced some more, and then they kissed so carelessly.

*****

Davy left Alana's room as discreetly as he could that next morning. She was in the deepest slumber; he knew he had to get out of there, and he had to be quick about it. He was back at the station within an hour. He tucked himself away on a bench at the end of the platform until his getaway train arrived. The night's events had left him shaken. The copious amount of alcohol consumed could have been partially to blame. Alana had left him feeling shipwrecked. He had no clue how he was going to get out of this one.

The trip home was arduous. The train had been diverted, which added an hour to his journey. It gave him time, though. He wished he could stay on it forever. He felt so safe despite the turgid journey.

Arriving home that evening, Davy sat himself down in front of his TV. He needed to unravel everything. He decided to sort through the mail found at the foot of his door when he got home. Among the flyers and credit card bills was a brown A4 envelope. It had no postage on it, so clearly had been hand-delivered. He stared at the sealed-down flap on the back of the envelope and then opened it gently.

The contents sent his head spinning. He became nauseous; sweat began to form on his brow. The envelope contained five A4 photographs of a naked Alana; she sat astride Davy on her hotel bed. He was naked also. He cupped his head in his hands; the phone rang. He let it ring a couple of more times, then answered.

'Davy!! Darling, how are you? How was your trip home?'

He recognised the voice.

'Alana, I don't understand. What is all this?'

'Oh, Davy sweetheart, now don't get all upset with me.'

He glanced at the photographs once more; they made him sick to the core.

'Now, I know that my silly old husband Harvey sent you to check on me. He is sooooo possessive and jealous!'

'With good reason!' Davy spat.

Davy's retort was met with giggles.

'Well, I like to have a good time, as you clearly found out, you naughty boy! However, I need to get Harvey off my back once and for all now. So, I am taking a bit of a risk here, but hey, I simply adore danger, it's so invigorating don't you think? Now, I want you to go and see him and put his mind at rest. I want you to tell him I have the virtue of a thousand nuns.'

'But these photos?' he quizzed.

'Well, I am appealing to your better nature here. If you don't tell Harvey that I am Julie Andrews personified, then I will make sure he gets to see the photos. At this point, I will disappear with a large chunk of his money which I have been carefully stashing. It will mean the well has dried up for me, but I'll soon find another mug. And as for you? Well, you will probably get a bullet in the head.'

Davy froze at those last words.

'A bullet?!'

Alana giggled briefly.

'You must know the sort of company Harvey keeps?'

Davy could guess.

'He knows some vicious people, Davy, my love. I guess when you have that sort of money, you need to know some people in dangerous places. The sort of people willing to look after your assets for you; precious assets, like me!'

'Why do you treat him like this?'

'Mainly boredom, Davy sweetie! I am sick of him sending guys like you after me. He is always doing it. It's annoying, especially when all I am doing is having fun! Truth is, I hate the man, but I simply adore his money; It's a dilemma, isn't it?'

Alana giggled again; the line then went silent. Davy heard a man's voice in the background. Clearly, she had moved on to her next conquest.

'So, there you have it, sweetie! You give me a glowing report, or you probably die. He has a hell of a temper when he wants. OK? Must dash … byeeeeeeeeeee!'

Davy looked again at the pictures; he wanted to wretch. A knuckle tapped at his front door. He nervously opened it to find a snowy-haired man; he spoke slow and low.

'Ah, Davy, I think we need a chat.'

Rachman wasn't alone. He was now sitting in front of Davy; his associate stood behind him. He was a man mountain. His head was closely shaved, and dark Gucci shades wrapped themselves around his eyes. His grey suit clung firmly to his muscly torso. Rachman cleared his throat to make way for his words,

> 'You have obviously realised that I know everything, Davy. It seems I am one step ahead of her, and you as it goes.'

Davy froze; Alana's giggle echoed in his head. His throat tightened, and his mouth grew dry. Rachman reached into his jacket. Placing a revolver on the desk, he looked at Davy and then nodded at the gun.

> 'Consider that your get-out clause, my friend. A clause with two simple options, kill Alana or simply kill yourself. Either way, you'll save me a job.'

As far as Davy was concerned, there was only one option.

Stitches

The bedroom walls shook to the music. It wasn't just any music, though; it was Marvin Gaye. Penny had always loved Marvin Gaye ever since she was a child. She remembered her mother playing his records whilst she sat playing with her toys. Yes, it was always Marvin Gaye and Roy Orbison. Penny had such fond memories of her mother from her childhood. She was always smiling and dancing, even though Penny's dad made her so unhappy. And so, the love of Marvin was handed down from mother to daughter.

The bedroom was part of the apartment she had shared with Matt. That was until he left her. It wasn't before time. He had been nothing but trouble, and the parting certainly wasn't amicable. Matt made it difficult for her after the split. She eventually got the divorce she so desperately wanted, though.

She stood in front of her wardrobe in her underwear, trying to choose something to wear. It was the last step in her preparations. She always thought of the whole 'getting ready' process as a sort of pagan ritual for her. She never liked being part of the game and never liked the idea of conforming with her peers. But since Matt left, she felt it necessary for her own survival. Like it or not, she had to take part in the game. She didn't want a relationship, though; not yet, anyway.

Penny picked a pink, long sleeve mini dress from the rail and slowly lowered herself into it. As she did so, she wondered what tonight would bring. Her aims were simple, drinks and dancing and then dancing and drinks. What more could she want? She fastened the dress as she checked her reflection in the mirror. Marvin was asking, 'What's goin' on?'. She was convinced there was something goin' on when Matt suggested they see other people. The weird thing was she agreed at first. She didn't think he'd do it. He was quite drunk when he made the suggestion. She said yes to humour him, thinking it was just a phase. Unfortunately, she stupidly left him to it. She didn't live up to the proposal, of course, but he began accusing her of seeing other people. Penny couldn't win. She remained faithful, put up with his nonsense, and then got abused for something she hadn't done. She felt angry more than hurt about it all; angry with herself.

She stepped into her shoes as the doorbell rang and then went downstairs to answer it. It was her old school friends Rosy and Monica.

'Almost ready!' she yelped,

'Give me a second to get my coat.'

'Tonight's the night, Penny! He'll be there waiting for you!' Monica teased.

'Who?' she replied.

'Mr Right, of course!' Monica replied.

She heard them both giggle as she put her coat on. That wasn't happening, though. Her interest in men couldn't be any lower. Seconds later, she slammed the front door firmly shut behind her. They were on their way.

*****

The festivities started in Maddigans. A few drinks would be had, and then they would go on to a club which was holding a Northern Soul night. Rosy was sourcing the drinks whilst Penny and Monica grabbed a table. Monica checked her phone, Penny raised her eyebrows as she looked on.

'He's not texted you I take it?'

'He' was Monica's boyfriend, Lenny. Not Penny's favourite person as he was a close friend of Matt's. She had to tolerate it until the day Lenny broke Monica's heart; she knew he would one day. Penny's cynicism and mistrust of most males grew day by day.

'I wasn't expecting him to. I was just checking the time,' Monica lied.

Penny smiled a rictus grin. Monica continued to steer the conversation on.

'Anyway, we are going to find you a new man tonight!'

'Not interested, Mon. I just want to have a few drinks and a dance.'

'You need to get back on the horse, girl! It's such a shame.'

'What is?'

'You and Matt. I never expected that.'

'It's the past, Monica. Let's leave it there now.'

'I always liked Matt, still do. I thought you were great together.'

'Whatever,' she replied.

'I always thought how lucky you were to capture him.'

'You make him sound like an escaped tiger,' Penny replied.

Monica pushed the topic further.

'I bet he was a bit of an animal, though!'

'He was dangerous, if that's what you mean, but not in the way you're suggesting.'

Penny was getting more agitated. She was there for a fun night out, not an inquest into her failed marriage. She needed to close down this avenue of discussion sharpish.

'Look, Monica, I can guess you are probably feeling split loyalties. I know Lenny and Matt are close. In fact, too close for my liking. You might want to keep an eye on Lenny. But other than that, let's fucking leave it!'

Rosy placed the cocktails on the table as Monica checked her phone again. Penny quickly grabbed her drink and downed it in one.

'Jesus, Penny!' exclaimed Rosy.

'I was thirsty, wasn't I? It's too bloody warm in this place too. Are we having the same again then? My round!'

Penny was off the starting blocks and bar-bound. Rosy turned to Monica.

'You been at her again, haven't you? Why won't you just let it lie? She's best rid of that loser, and the sooner you get that, the better for us all!'

'I think you're wrong, and she's mad. Matt is a lovely guy.'

'Well, that helps, doesn't it?' Rosy scolded.

Monica shrugged her shoulders.

'What?'

'I'm not daft. The times I have seen you go all giggly whenever he was around.'

'You're talking bollocks, Rosy.'

'Of course I am. Look, if you know what's good for you, you'll stay away from Matt. What would Lenny say for a start off?'

The subject was closed immediately; for now, anyway.

*****

Shangri-la's presented a much-needed soul groove to the trio. The vinyl spun feverishly on the turntables. The sounds were authentic, soulful and loud. The girls sat at the back of the club. Several empty glasses filled their little table, along with three half-filled ones. Penny was in her element now.

'Can you hear that?' she shouted to her two friends.

'Yeah, sounds great,' Monica replied.

'No, I don't think you get it. What do you hear?'

Monica was puzzled.

'Music, stupid!' she replied.

'No, it's not just music. It's musicians, not computers. Every note you hear has been physically played and recorded by human beings. It's real, not plastic.'

Monica never appreciated Penny's love for music, well, not to that level anyway. A tune was just a tune. As long as she could shake her pants to it; that was all she needed. Arthur Conley's 'Sweet Soul Music' was up next. Penny jumped from her chair and hit the dance floor; Rosy followed. They both executed perfect Northern Soul dance steps to the tune. Penny was back in her zone, eyes closed as she shook her body. This was what she called getting back on the horse; not wasting her time on any man. The Trammps' 'Hold Back the Night' was next; she couldn't stop. The rhythm infected everyone on the dancefloor. The fever was building, and Penny's endorphins were having a blast. The song came to its climax. Penny stood gasping to herself. Beads of sweat found their way down her back. This was living. She turned to Rosy; her smile was as wide as an ocean. Rosy was frozen still. Her face was fixed on the other side of the room. Matt stood at the bar; he wasn't alone.

*****

'Alright, Penny? Looking good.' teased Matt.

Monica was oblivious to her friend, who was standing behind her, glaring back at Matt.

'Can I get you a drink?' he laughed.

'I want nothing from you, and as for you, Monica, what the hell do you think you're doing?'

'Just catching up with Matt here. I haven't seen him in ages.'

Penny couldn't believe her friend's words. An inferno of rage started in her stomach.

'Why are you talking to this piece of shit?'

'What am I doing wrong, Penny?! I'm just saying hello to Matt.'

'And what will Lenny think about this?!'

'If you must know, we have split up. I dumped him a few days ago.'

The news sent Penny reeling for a second. She recovered, though.

'So now you got your eyes on this lowlife? Is that it?!'

'Well, you're done with him now, aren't you?'

Monica moved alongside Matt and put her arm around him.

'Seems a shame to see him alone. You don't know what you lost, girl.'

Matt smirked. Cats and pots of cream came to mind.

Penny stood tall.

'You are making such a big mistake if you are seriously thinking of getting involved with him. I only hope you don't regret this.'

'Look, I don't want to fall out with you,' Monica advised.

'Bit late for that, I think!'

'Piss off then and leave us alone!' Monica shouted.

Penny turned on her heels and headed back to a vigilant Rosy. As Penny got closer to her, Rosy just shook her head from side to side.

'Unbelievable, Penny. I did warn her.'

'You knew about this?' Penny asked.

'I found out tonight. I thought it was just a fascination, but she's gone for it, and in full view. That woman has no fucking shame.'

'She's going to regret it so much.'

'I thought you were done with him?' asked Rosy.

'Oh, I am. I'm done with men in general. But this isn't good.'

Penny reached for her coat; Rosy did the same. They hurriedly left the club; Monica smiled on and threw a teasing wave at them.

*****

Chip Alley was as lively as ever for a Saturday night. Revellers bounced around the street, some of them ricocheting drunkenly off the walls. There was laughter and singing, accompanied by arguing and pushing. It was the sound of the human condition having a good time. Penny and Rosy had hit a few bars after leaving Shangri-la's and now found themselves in need of kebabs and chips. Penny was still fuming at Monica's underhand moves. Rosy persuaded her that a kebab might make her feel better; temporarily at least.

They queued at the door of the kebab house. The people ahead of them were all busy staring at their mobiles. People were sending texts of love and hate from the shop up into the ether. Penny looked at them and wondered why they were bothering at all. No one cared at the end of the day. Rosy shook her out of her apathy.

'What are you having, Penny? I could kill a lamb doner with all the sauce and salad!'

'I'm not really hungry.'

'You are, but you don't know it. How about chicken curry off the floor?'

Rosy laughed at her own words as Penny grinned politely. She couldn't let Monica get involved with Matt. It just couldn't happen.

They both sat on the kerbside eating their food. Rosy demolished her kebab; Penny picked at her curry and rice. She heard a familiar laugh and looked up. Monica was heading down the road arm in arm with Matt.

Penny dropped her food into the gutter and got to her feet quickly. Rosy remained seated on the hard stone.

'She's not worth it, Penny! Ignore her and sit back down.'

Penny hurtled herself toward Monica. Matt grabbed Monica and sidestepped her past Penny. Penny turned and grabbed Monica's arm so tightly that her jacket sleeve tore.

'You stupid bitch, Penny!' Monica screamed,

'That's going to need stitching! You can pay for that, you idiot!'

Penny pulled her jacket off and raised the sleeve of her pink dress.

'Just like I paid for these?!' she countered.

Monica stared at a scar on the top of Penny's arm. Matt's face flushed. He briskly walked away. Tears formed in the two women's eyes.

'Matt did that to you?' she asked.

Penny nodded.

'I don't believe you!'

'It's true, Mon,' chipped in Rosy.

'You knew, Rosy? Then why didn't you tell me?'

'It's too painful for me,' said Penny.

Penny reached out for Monica and held her close. 'And that's why I am not going to let what happened to me happen to you.'

The passers-by navigated their way around the three women and their group hug.

Sad Songs

Billy Rose's mood wasn't getting any better as the session went on. He propped his Cuban heels up on the sofa in the control room. The bangles around his wrist rattled as he swept his long hair back. He scratched at his goatee beard and sighed. Staring at the red light above the door to the vocal booth, he wondered why she couldn't get the vocals right. Frankie stood on the other side of the door, singing away. The pop shield stood between her luscious lips and the microphone. The headphones clung to her head for dear life. She knew they'd spent too much time recording the track, but she was now past the point of caring.

It was the last of three tracks Billy wanted to present to a local management company. The first two had been recorded painlessly. Bass and drums had been recorded for the last track. The respective musicians involved had bunked off to the pub. This left Billy to lay down the guitars and Frankie the vocals. It wasn't going well, though. Frankie and Billy had argued. He had experienced problems keeping his guitar in tune. He blamed the temperature of the room. She was growing sick of the sight of him.

Gizmo was engineering the session, but Billy didn't like him. He didn't like him because he knew what he was doing, and that meant Billy couldn't pull any bullshit on him. The simple truth was that Billy wanted complete control. Frankie knew the tracks would suffer if he was left to run the session. She exited the vocal booth.

'I can't do it any better than that, at least not tonight.' Billy shook his head.

'I don't get why you are having trouble with this track. You know it inside out. You sing it well every gig we play. What's the problem?'

'Not now, Billy, I'm done in.'

Gizmo lowered his head over the mixing desk, ducking from the imminent crossfire.

'Done in? What the fuck does that mean? You're a professional, so get back in there and do it again.'

'You don't own me, Billy, and you certainly don't control me! So fucking do one!'

And that was it. She simply walked out of the door and didn't reckon she would return any time soon.

She trudged her way down Bute Street towards town. It was time for a drink; more importantly, it was time for a think. Day and night had long crossed each other with a kiss and a handshake. Light raindrops fell, their form being caught by the amber streetlights. The roads hissed with the passing traffic as her heels clip-clopped her way down the street. She was wondering where to go; she certainly didn't want to catch up with the rest of the band. She had grown as sick of them as she had Billy. *Maddigans was the favourite,* she thought. The two guys on the door were nice enough, if not a little rough around the edges. As she neared the club, she could hear a busker nearby, and she thought of him. She wondered what he was doing now and who he might be with. The bouncers smiled as she walked by. Ten minutes later, she had two Jägerbombs under her belt. Benevolence became her as she sat back and smiled.

*****

He had caught up with her. Billy Rose stood over Frankie, his hands were clenched, but his words were soft.

'What's wrong, Frankie? Talk to me.'

She just shook her head. She looked at her empty glass and then at the bar. She smiled at the red-haired girl stood behind it. She smiled back and then nodded as she prepared another drink for Frankie.

'Getting drunk ain't the answer, girl,' he nagged.

'But it's rock and roll, Billy, isn't it? Cigarettes and alcohol and all that!'

He knew. He could tell it was done, both their relationship and the band. He also knew they both harboured guilt. The Wonderwall kid was a nice guy and didn't deserve what they had both done to him. Frankie had often wondered if he had worked out their betrayal. Either way, he didn't deserve the heartbreak she had inflicted on him. Billy just regarded him as collateral damage in a love war; shit happened after all.

'You still love him, don't you?' he taunted.

'Go away, Billy. I told you I'm done.'

'Well, I'm not!'

'Don't you feel anything at all? He looked up to you. He almost hero worshipped you.'

'I can't get attached to that kind of shit.'

'But you got attached to me? We ran off and left him. We disappeared out of his life. That must have been awful for him.'

'Oh please, I'll get my violin, shall I?'

'You're a complete bastard, Billy Rose!'

Frankie rose and headed to the bar to collect her drink. Billy tagged along.

'So, what you gonna do now? Try and find him? Well, that won't be difficult. He's probably out there now on the street, the musical prostitute that he is!'

'That's not fair. He's good at what he does, he provides pleasure, and he makes people smile and feel good. And he's a great musician!'

'He's a sell-out, pure and simple.'

'Oh, just fuck off, Billy. You looked at yourself lately? Still chasing the dream. You're a joke! It's over, Billy, face it!'

But he couldn't accept her words. He was going to keep on keeping on. He was driven by one fear, and that was having to live with a dead dream. That couldn't happen. He simply had to keep going. Frankie took a swig of her drink and gave him one last glance. She spoke softly and almost sympathetically.

'Go, Billy, please.'

He shrugged his shoulders and left the building.

*****

Bickle stood against his car, sipping at a coffee. He viewed the passing throng as Brian the Spike sidled up to him.

'Busy, innit?' Brian stated.

'It's Saturday night, Brian. Of course, it's busy.'

'Just making conversation, that's all.'

The two men stood in silence, watching the nightlife unfold in front of them. Bickle never ceased to be amazed at the effervescence of the street at night.

'Look at them all.'

'Yeah, some lookers out there tonight!'

'Listen to yourself. I didn't mean that. They are all out there, lovers, fighters, the heartbroken and heartbreakers.'

'Bit deep for me, Bickle mate. Had any good fares tonight?' Brian asked.

'Nothing special. They were all mostly drunk and comatose, of course. A lot of self-medication goes on out there at night.'

'Bit cynical that.'

Bickle continued.

'No, I'm just saying, there's a lot of fractured people out there.'

Brian the Spike shrugged.

'I guess so. Just life, innit?'

Bickle thought of her and how she left him. Eleri was married, of course, they always were. Bickle had fallen deeply in love with her, but she was betrothed to a copper. It could only end badly for him, possibly for everyone. And then it did. Eleri was killed in a car crash on her way home after seeing him. It had been some years since, but the guilt still lived within him. Some of the cabbies were familiar with the scenario, but no one judged Bickle.

'Anyway, how are you doing?' asked Brian the Spike.

'I'm getting there, thanks. It's been a bit of a long road. I know I'll be glad to finish tonight, that's for sure. There's been some crazy shit going on. Did you hear about that trouble in Grangetown? And the car crash on the A4232?'

'I heard a guy collapsed in the Frantic Fox earlier. I don't think it ended well.'

'It was Spanish Ianto,' Bickle stated solemnly.

'Fuck! No way?!'

'Yeah.' Bickle shrugged.

'How do you know?'

'Jungle drums, innit, you know this place. It may be a city, but it's a small one.'

'Poor Ianto.'

They both stood in an almost spontaneous silence in honour of the deceased man. Bickle heard the clip-clop of a woman's heels. He looked up at a slightly inebriated woman. She wore a leather jacket and trousers. The jacket hung loosely around her shoulders.

'You free?' she drawled.

Bickle gallantly opened the back door of his cab for her.

*****

Frankie stood nervously at the steps of the flat. She could hear the music inside. She identified the Rolling Stones' 'Sympathy For The Devil' as its chords chugged along. He was obviously home. The Jägerbombs were wearing off, and her throat was drying up. Her nerves stood on end. There was a decision to be made, and she knew she had been procrastinating for far too long. Should she text him or simply knock on the door? It was a hard call. Things had to be considered. What if he wasn't alone? What if he didn't want to see her ever again? What if he simply hated her now?

She paced up and down between the flat and the street corner. The more she sobered up, the more she threw questions at herself. Why did she leave him? She loved the Wonderwall Kid, but marriage scared her, and Billy Rose tempted her. Frankie's affair with Billy had started before she left the Wonderwall Kid. He never suspected a thing, or at least that's what she thought. More questions popped up; what if he did know about their affair? Maybe that's why he proposed. Maybe it was a last desperate attempt to make sure she never left him for Billy. Frankie wrestled with her conscience and guilt. If the Wonderwall Kid knew about their affair, he must have really loved her when he asked her to marry him. She thought hard. That would have been some gesture made with a giant leap of faith. The more she thought about it, the more she thought he couldn't have known anything.

Frankie found herself at the steps to the flat once more. She bit the bullet. She chose text as her medium.

'Are you home?'

The curtains twitched above her head; the front door opened shortly after.

*****

He poured the wine slowly. Frankie flicked through his vinyl collection as if she had never been away.

'Why are you here, Frankie?'

'Everyone's got to be somewhere, I guess.'

He almost smiled at her words. She took the record out of the sleeve. She had picked Dylan's 'Blood on the Tracks'. She always had taste; it was a great choice, of course.

The first chords of 'Tangled up in Blue' sounded out.

'I missed you. That's why I am here.'

'Wow, I'm touched.'

'I know I hurt you.'

'Hurt me?!' he threw back.

'I know, I know, I'm sorry.'

'You know what I don't get? I don't get how funny it was that both you and Billy Rose disappeared from my life in a heartbeat. His band seemed to stop doing the circuit too. All very strange.

At that moment, Dylan broke into 'Simple Twist of Fate'. The irony wasn't lost on either of them.

Frankie's face reddened. The Wonderwall Kid was shocked by his awakening.

'You were fucking him, weren't you?!'

Frankie grew uncomfortable, but he deserved the truth.

'Ok, that's why I am here. I have been haunted by the ghost of our relationship for some time.'

'And?'

'Yes, it was true. We had started seeing each other before you and I split up. Your proposal defined the situation for me, and I ran. I gave you a load of bullshit excuses and legged it. And there isn't a day goes by that I don't regret it.'

'Why him?'

'He can be a very persuasive guy, I guess. And it was exciting. I know that's not what you want to hear. I am so so sorry.'

Dylan moved on to 'You're a Big Girl Now'. Silence fell over both of them as he sang his words. The Wonderwall Kid gently broke the silence.

'You know the stupidest thing of all? I still love you. I never stopped.'

'I have been waiting a long time to hear those words again.'

They kissed. Frankie then took his hand and led him to the bedroom.

The Wonderwall Kid felt a seed of forgiveness sprouting within. He hoped he was doing the right thing.

Tickets to Ride

The day's first train to London snaked alongside platform one. Jimmy the Jump Guy checked his ticket, which told him he had a seat in carriage D. He knew he wouldn't be using it, though. He never liked being told what to do or where to go; *all part of his free spirit*, he figured. He took a place in the vestibule between carriages D and E. The heavy train door was slammed behind him by the train guard. The service wasn't a busy one, and he knew seating was pretty free, but he wanted to stand. He needed to think; he knew he was just running away again, but running away was ok, wasn't it?

He wasn't sure why he chose London as his destination that morning. He knew people there, of course; he knew people everywhere. He knew he didn't want to go back home to Manchester, though. He was sure of that. He'd be alright. He always landed on his feet, but it was usually alone. Scrutinising his thoughts, he stared at the platform as the train hit Newport. Mostly empty, apart from a few stragglers getting their train home after a heavy night. Overthinking was a bad thing for him; Jasper always told him that. It didn't stop him from doing it. Reflecting on the night before, he thought of Brandii's touch. She was a sweet girl and a few years younger than him. He felt bad leaving her like that. She'd professed her love for him, and he threw it back at her with some small disdain. It didn't make him feel good.

The rain had begun to fall, and raindrops crept down the train windows, coming to a watery ending at the bottom of them. What had been the point of any of this? What had been the point of any of his life come to that? He had just cruised through it, although sometimes the sea could get rough. But he hadn't made any plans. He just let life take him on the journey. The few decisions he had made in life had defined him. He felt they had turned him into nothing but a coward and a quitter. But he was about to open a new chapter in his life. He hoped for an opportunity to make amends, to obtain absolution from some higher power.

*****

Kylie wandered down the aisles of the train from carriage to carriage. His head was in a total mindfuck. He couldn't believe his dad was gone in the blink of an eye. He couldn't believe the thread that we all hang on was so thin. The fragility of life was far from embracing, but the walls of mortality will always crumble and fall in the end. Maeve had given him some kind words, but they were never going to be more than scant comfort. He wasn't sure if he should call his mother. But she may have moved on again. He hadn't heard from her in a while. He just hoped someone back home would contact her. He wasn't ready for the bullshit his mother would no doubt spout at him either.

He continued walking up and down the corridors. The train wasn't busy, but he didn't want to sit in any one place. His agitation was getting the better of him. He passed a young mother with her crying baby. She gently stroked the baby's face as it calmed down; Kylie felt envy. Oh, to have that nurturing when he was a child; to have some level of love and care. He felt sad, angry, and hopeless all at once. The very absence of caring parents had probably led him to his itinerant and devious ways. It was hard for him not to play the victim now. Ducking and diving his way through life was the norm. He had no time for relationships. He was always moving or, more than likely, running. He had to get out of town. He needed to keep his head down for a bit. He found himself in carriage D, the ticket inspector walked towards him.

'Tickets, please!'

Kylie turned to go the other way, but his passage was blocked by the woman with the baby. She held a clean nappy in her hand. He turned back to face the ticket inspector and gulped.

*****

The train threw itself into the Severn Tunnel. Darkness would envelop it for the next four miles. Jimmy continued his stare into the blackness. He turned his thoughts to what he would do in London when he got there. He had a mate in Ladbroke Grove who ran a small café. He would probably go and pester him first. The carriage door swished open, and a woman with a baby walked through. She looked at Jimmy and smiled.

'It's all kicking off in there!'

As she locked herself in the toilet, Jimmy poked his head into the carriage. He saw a ticket inspector being a bit heavy-handed with a young guy. The guy looked agitated. Jimmy walked towards them as the ticket inspector spoke.

> 'I've heard it all before, young man! You aren't the first to tell me you've lost your ticket somewhere on the train.'
>
> 'But I'm telling the truth,' Kylie protested.
>
> 'Unless you have some proof you have bought a ticket, you'll have to buy one off me now or get off at the next stop!'

Jimmy recognised the desperation in Kylie's eyes. The youngster looked shot through.

> 'Hey, give the kid a break!' he shouted.
>
> 'Stay out of this, sir, if you don't mind,' the ticket man advised.

Kylie was getting ever more fractious.

'I don't believe this. I have to get to London, but I don't have any more money!'

'Then you'll have to get off at Bristol Parkway as I advised you.'

Jimmy couldn't let this go any further.

'How much to keep you from chucking this guy off the train?'

The ticket man looked at Jimmy with incredulity.

'What?! Do you know this young man then?'

'Maybe I do, maybe I don't. You needn't worry about that, though, do you? How much?' Jimmy replied.

The guard pressed a few buttons on his hand-held device.

'Fifty-two pounds eighty.'

Jimmy pulled a wad of notes from his pocket.

'I'd prefer card, sir, if you can?'

Jimmy peeled off fifty-five pounds in notes and waved them in the guard's face,

'Keep the change!'

The guard hastily printed the ticket out. He walked away, unsure who really won the battle.

*****

'Man, that was one of the nicest things anyone has ever done for me,' gushed Kylie.

'I'm amazed how you got on the train without a ticket?' Jimmy replied.

'I didn't! I lost it when I got on!'

Jimmy laughed.

'Never bullshit a bullshitter, kid.'

'Sorry, I just needed to get away from home.'

'Where you from then?'

'Cardiff.'

'Me too, well, not originally. I moved down from Manchester years back. But my time is done in Cardiff now.'

'Moving on? Yeah, me too.'

'Not sure if I am moving on or running away, to be honest,' Jimmy informed.

A brief silence fell between them. Jimmy was finding himself being dragged into one of those tell-all situations. A moment when you gladly tell all your secrets and woes to a stranger. Kylie felt he had found a kindred spirit. It gave him brief hope. Jimmy pulled out a hip flask and handed it to Kylie.

'Fancy a nip? It's the water of life, apparently.'

Kylie smiled as he took the vessel. The whisky hit his stomach and settled with a warmth he hadn't felt in a while. Jimmy frowned as he took in Kylie's visage.

'You look familiar.'

'I've been about a bit,' he joked.

'You go out in town much?'

'I do a lot of work in the community at night,' Kylie teased.

'I've seen you somewhere. You go in Maddigans at all?'

'Now and then. My ex works behind the bar.'

Jimmy left it there. He wondered if Kylie's ex was his mate Jasper's new beau. She could very well be the same person. They decided to exchange names, Kylie fist-bumping Jimmy as they did so.

'What are you running from then, Jimmy?'

Jimmy gulped, but he figured it would be ok to offload; who knows, he might even feel better for it. He held back his story,

'You got a family, Kylie?'

'I did have. My mum fucked off years ago with another bloke. And then to cap it all, my dad dropped dead last night.'

'Jesus! Kylie, that's fucked, man!'

'Tell me about it. I keep hoping it's all a bad dream. That's why I am here now. Well, that's not strictly the only reason. I am wanted and not by the Old Bill. Some unsavoury people want a chat with me about something.'

'How unsavoury are we talking?'

'Put it this way, I'd probably struggle walking for a while if they caught up with me.'

Jimmy paused for thought for a moment. Kylie took another swig from the hip flask. They were both shaken briefly as the train charged over a set of rail points. Jimmy pressed a little more.

'So, your dad? What happened there?'

'He basically dropped down dead from his bar stool in the Frantic Fox. I don't know what caused it, although I have a couple of friends I can get hold of to find out once I get to where I am going.'

'Which is where?' Jimmy asked.

'Fucked if I know!'

They laughed in unison. Kylie felt relaxed despite his dilemma.

'What's your story then?' he asked.

'Women and a lack of self-belief that I'll ever be happy with one. I want to settle down, but I know it's pointless. I'm a commitment-phobe, plain and simple.'

'Aren't all men?' Kylie teased.

'I had a woman tell me she loved me last night. I've known her for a while. Nice girl, but as soon as she said that, I had me Adidas on, and I was off!'

Kylie howled. Jimmy continued,

'I don't think she was happy about it, but I had to go.'

'Still, that's cool, man. To have a woman tell you she loves you, that's precious; you might regret it one day mind.'

'I am already, but I'm afraid,' Jimmy confessed.

'Of?'

'Getting hurt.'

Kylie nodded silently.

Jimmy continued.

'I got a daughter back up north. The last time I saw her, she was only three. She'll be eighteen soon.'

'And you never hear from her?'

'Yes I do, but I never answer her calls … because I don't know what to say and because I am scared…and a fucking coward too I guess.'

'She wants to get to know you, obviously. She wouldn't be calling for any other reason. Count yourself lucky, man. My mum didn't want to know, and as for my dad? Well, it's too late for that now. It's too late for him and me. But you, well, maybe you need to answer that call next time?'

Jimmy looked through the window at the rain. It was hitting the train harder now.

'Yeah, maybe I do.'

*****

'You got a defibrillator for these?' Jimmy teased the man behind the bar.

The beers were lifeless. Two livelier replacements were placed on the bar post-haste. Jimmy hated London pubs, but Kylie was enjoying every minute.

'So, this is it, the Big Smoke!'
Jimmy grinned,
'First time, is it?'
'I came up as a kid on a school trip once. Never been back.'
'And you definitely want to stay here for now?'
'I have to, Jimmy. I told you.'
In the short time that Jimmy had known Kylie, he had grown fond of him, and more importantly, wanted to protect him.
'Gimme your mobile number. I got something for you.'
Within minutes Jimmy had shared his contact in Ladbrook Grove with Kylie. Jimmy nodded at the phone as Kylie looked at it.
'That's a mate of mine, got a café not far from here. It's ok, I have told him to expect you. He owes me. Do yourself a favour and keep your head down. He'll probably have you waiting tables or something. At least it's clean, honest work for now, and that's what you need until you sort your shit out.'
Kylie didn't know what to do. He threw his arms around Jimmy.
'Thanks, Jimmy. I don't know how to thank you!'
'Just keep your fucking head down. That's all I ask. I'll stay in touch.'
'And what about you, Jimmy? What are you going to do?'
'The right thing, I guess.'

*****

Jimmy stepped off the train. The Cardiff sky threatened more rain. Feeling lazy, he took the lift to the ground floor. It had been an emotional day for him, the climax being his decision to come back, his decision to stop running. He exited the station at the rear and walked out onto Penarth Road. Brandii ran to him as soon as she saw him. It was time to try and settle, to give things a chance. It was time to give himself a chance. Brandii hugged him tightly. He felt his phone go off in his pocket and checked it. He answered.

'Hello?'

'Hi, Dad, it's me!'

The End

Many thanks for your time, why not sign up to my Blog?

https://michaeljphillips.co.uk/

Thanks again

Mike

Printed in Great Britain
by Amazon